The Irregular at Magic High School

UPHEAVAL PROLOGUE ARC II

22

Tsutomu Sato

Illustration Kana Ishida

NEW YORK

THE IRREGULAR AT MAGIC HIGH SCHOOL
TSUTOMU SATO

Translation by Kenia A. Hara
Cover art by Kana Ishida

This book is a work of fiction. Names, characters, places, and incidents are the product of the author's imagination or are used fictitiously. Any resemblance to actual events, locales, or persons, living or dead, is coincidental.

MAHOUKA KOUKOU NO RETTOUSEI Vol. 22
©Tsutomu Sato 2017
Edited by Dengeki Bunko
First published in Japan in 2017 by KADOKAWA CORPORATION, Tokyo.
English translation rights arranged with KADOKAWA CORPORATION, Tokyo, through Tuttle-Mori Agency, Inc., Tokyo.

English translation © 2024 by Yen Press, LLC

Yen Press, LLC supports the right to free expression and the value of copyright. The purpose of copyright is to encourage writers and artists to produce the creative works that enrich our culture.

The scanning, uploading, and distribution of this book without permission is a theft of the author's intellectual property. If you would like permission to use material from the book (other than for review purposes), please contact the publisher. Thank you for your support of the author's rights.

Yen On
150 West 30th Street, 19th Floor
New York, NY 10001

Visit us at yenpress.com
facebook.com/yenpress
twitter.com/yenpress
yenpress.tumblr.com
instagram.com/yenpress

First Yen On Edition: May 2024
Edited by Yen On Editorial: Ivan Liang
Designed by Yen Press Design: Wendy Chan

Yen On is an imprint of Yen Press, LLC.
The Yen On name and logo are trademarks of Yen Press, LLC.

The publisher is not responsible for websites (or their content) that are not owned by the publisher.

Library of Congress Cataloging-in-Publication Data
Names: Sato, Tsutomu. | Ishida, Kana, illustrator.
Title: The irregular at Magic High School / Tsutomu Sato ; Illustrations by Kana Ishida.
Other titles: Mahōka kōkō no rettosei. English
Description: First Yen On edition. | New York, NY : Yen On, 2016–
Identifiers: LCCN 2015042401 | ISBN 9780316348805 (v 1 : pbk.) | ISBN 9780316390293 (v. 2 : pbk.) | ISBN 9780316390309 (v. 3 : pbk.) | ISBN 9780316390316 (v. 4 : pbk.) | ISBN 9780316390323 (v. 5 : pbk.) | ISBN 9780316390330 (v. 6 : pbk.) | ISBN 9781975300074 (v. 7 : pbk.) | ISBN 9781975327125 (v. 8 : pbk.) | ISBN 9781975327149 (v. 9 : pbk.) | ISBN 9781975327163 (v. 10 : pbk.) | ISBN 9781975327187 (v. 11 : pbk.) | ISBN 9781975327200 (v. 12 : pbk.) | ISBN 9781975332327 (v. 13 : pbk.) | ISBN 9781975332471 (v. 14 : pbk.) | ISBN 9781975332495 (v. 15 : pbk.) | ISBN 9781975332518 (v. 16 : pbk.) | ISBN 9781975332532 (v. 17 : pbk.) | ISBN 9781975332556 (v. 18 : pbk.) | ISBN 9781975343835 (v. 19 : pbk.) | ISBN 9781975345167 (v. 20 : pbk.) | ISBN 9781975345181 (v. 21 : pbk.) | ISBN 9781975345204 (v. 22 : pbk.) |
Subjects: CYAC: Brothers and sisters—Fiction. | Magic—Fiction. | High schools—Fiction. | Schools—Fiction. | Japan—Fiction. | Science fiction.
Classification: LCC PZ7.1.S265 Ir 2016 | DDC [Fic]—dc23
LC record available at http://lccn.loc.gov/2015042401

ISBNs: 978-1-9753-4520-4 (paperback)
978-1-9753-4521-1 (ebook)

Printing 1, 2024

LSC-C

Printed in the United States of America

UPHEAVAL PROLOGUE ARC II

An irregular older brother with a certain flaw.
An honor roll younger sister who is perfectly flawless.
When the two siblings enrolled in Magic High School,
a dramatic life unfolded—

Character

Tatsuya Shiba

Class 3-E.
Approaches everything in a detached manner. His sister Miyuki's Guardian.

Miyuki Shiba

Class 3-A. Tatsuya's younger sister; enrolled as the top student last year. Specializes in freezing magic. Dotes on her older brother.

Leonhard Saijou

Class 3-F. Tatsuya's friend. Course 2 student. Specializes in hardening magic. Has a cheerful personality.

Erika Chiba

Class 3-F. Tatsuya's friend. Course 2 student. A charming troublemaker.

Mizuki Shibata

Class 3-E. Tatsuya's friend. Has pushion-radiation sensitivity. Serious and a bit of an airhead.

Mikihiko Yoshida

Class 3-B. From a famous family that uses old magic. Has known Erika since they were children.

Honoka Mitsui

Class 3-A. Miyuki's classmate. Specializes in light-wave vibration magic. Impulsive when emotional.

Shizuku Kitayama

Class 3-A. Miyuki's classmate. Specializes in vibration and acceleration magic. Doesn't show emotional ups and downs very much.

Subaru Satomi

Class 3-D. Frequently mistaken for a pretty boy. Cheerful and easy to get along with.

Eimi "Amelia Goldie" Akechi

Class 3-B. A quarter Japanese. Almost everyone calls her "Amy." Daughter of the prominent Goldie family.

Akaha Sakurakouji

Class 3-B. Friends with Subaru and Amy. Wears gothic lolita clothes and loves theme parks.

Shun Morisaki

Class 3-A. Miyuki's classmate. Specializes in CAD quick-draw. Takes great pride in being a Course 1 student.

Hagane Tomitsuka

Class 3-E. A magic martial arts user with the nickname "Range Zero." Uses magic martial arts.

Mayumi Saegusa

An alum. Currently attends Magic University. Has a devilish personality but weak when on the defensive.

Azusa Nakajou

An alum. Former student council president. Shy and has trouble expressing herself.

Suzune Ichihara

An alum. Currently a student at Magic University. Calm, collected, and book smart.

Hanzou Gyoubu-Shoujou Hattori

An alum. Former head of the club committee. Gifted but can be too serious at times.

Mari Watanabe

An alum. Mayumi's good friend. Well-rounded and often sporting for a fight.

Katsuto Juumonji

An alum. Currently a student at Magic University. "A boulder-like person," according to Tatsuya.

Koutarou Tatsumi

An alum and former member of the disciplinary committee. Has a heroic and dynamic personality.

Isao Sekimoto

An alum and former member of the disciplinary committee. Lost the Thesis Competition. Committed acts of espionage.

Midori Sawaki

An alum. Former member of the disciplinary committee. Has a complex about his girlish name.

Takeaki Kirihara

An alum. Junior High Kanto Kenjutsu Tournament champion.

Kei Isori

An alum. Former student council treasurer. Excels in magical theory. Engaged to Kanon.

Sayaka Mibu

An alum. Placed second in the nation at the girl's Junior High Kendo Tournament.

Kanon Chiyoda

An alum. Former chairwoman of the disciplinary committee. As confrontational as her predecessor, Mari.

Kasumi Saegusa

A junior. Mayumi Saegusa's younger sister. Izumi's older twin sister. Has a cheerful and feisty personality.

Takuma Shippou

A junior. Eldest son of the Shippou family, one of the families with excellent magicians and a new addition to the Ten Master Clans.

Izumi Saegusa

A junior. Mayumi Saegusa's younger sister. Kasumi's younger twin sister. Has a meek and gentle personality.

Minami Sakurai

A junior. Presents herself as Tatsuya and Miyuki's cousin. A Guardian candidate for Miyuki.

Kento Smith

A junior. A Caucasian boy whose parents are naturalized Japanese citizens from the USNA.

Koharu Hirakawa

An alum. Participated as an engineer in the Nine School Competition. Withdrew from the Thesis Competition.

Chiaki Hirakawa

A senior. Holds enmity toward Tatsuya.

Shiina Mitsuya

A new student enrolled at First High. Always wears custom earmuffs due to her keen sense of hearing.

Saburou Yaguruma

Shiina's childhood friend and self-proclaimed bodyguard.

Haruka Ono

A general counselor of First High. Tends to get bullied but has another side to her personality.

Yakumo Kokonoe

A user of an ancient magic called *ninjutsu*. Tatsuya's martial arts master.

Satomi Asuka

First High nurse. Male students love her calm and warm smile.

Kazuo Tsuzura

First High teacher. Specializes in magic geometry. Manages the Thesis Competition team.

Jennifer Smith

A Caucasian woman naturalized as a Japanese citizen. Teaches Tatsuya's class and magic engineering classes.

Tomoko Chikura

An alum. Competed in the women's solo Shields Down, an event at the Nine School Competition.

Tsugumi Igarashi

An alum. Former biathlon club president.

Yousuke Igarashi

A senior. Tsugumi's younger brother. Has a somewhat reserved personality.

Kerry Minakami

An alum. Male representative for the main Monolith Code, an event at the Nine School Competition.

Kumiko Kunisaki

An alum. Amy's teammate in the Rower and Gunner event at the Nine School Competition. Has a frank personality.

Masaki Ichijou
A senior at Third High. Direct heir to the Ichijou family, one of the Ten Master Clans.

Gouki Ichijou
Masaki's father. Current head of the Ichijou family, one of the Ten Master Clans.

Shinkurou Kichijouji
A senior at Third High. Also known as Cardinal George.

Midori Ichijou
Masaki's mother. Warm and good at cooking.

Akane Ichijou
Eldest Ichijou daughter. Masaki's younger sister. A junior in middle school. Likes Shinkurou.

Ushio Kitayama
Shizuku's father. Big shot in the business world. His business name is Ushio Kitagata.

Benio Kitayama
Shizuku's mother. An A-rank magician who was once renowned for her vibration magic.

Ruri Ichijou
Second Ichijou daughter. Masaki's younger sister. A put-together girl who marches to the beat of her own drum.

Wataru Kitayama
Shizuku's younger brother. Just started middle school. Dearly loves his older sister. Aims to be a magic engineer.

Harumi Naruse
Shizuku's older cousin. Student at National Magic University Fourth Affiliated High School.

Pixie
A home helper robot belonging to Magic High School. Official name 3H (Humanoid Home Helper: a human-shaped chore-assisting robot) Type P94.

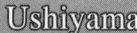

Ushiyama
Manager of Four Leaves Technology's CAD R&D Section 3. Has earned Tatsuya's trust.

Toshikazu Chiba
Erika Chiba's eldest brother. Deceased. Worked at the Ministry of Police.

Ernst Rosen
A prominent CAD manufacturer. President of Rosen Magicraft's Japanese branch.

Naotsugu Chiba
Erika Chiba's second-eldest brother. Mari's lover. Possesses full mastery of the Chiba (thousand blades) style of kenjutsu. Nicknamed "Kirin-Child of the Chiba."

Retsu Kudou
Renowned as the strongest magician in the world. Given the honorary title of Sage.

Inagaki
Deceased. When he was alive, he worked as an inspector at the Ministry of Police and was Toshikazu Chiba's subordinate.

Makoto Kudou
Son of Retsu Kudou, elder of Japan's magic world, and current head of the Kudou family.

Anna Rosen Katori
Erika's mother. Half Japanese and half German, was the mistress of Erika's father, the current leader of the Chiba.

Minoru Kudou
Makoto's son. Second year at the National Magic University Second Affiliated High School, but barely attends due to frequent illness. Also Kyouko Fujibayashi's younger brother by a different father.

Mamoru Kuki
One of the Eighteen Support Clans. Follows the Kudou family. Calls Retsu Kudou "Sensei" out of respect.

Maki Sawamura
An impressive actress nominated as best female lead for distinguished film awards. Acknowledged for both her beauty and acting skills.

Harunobu Kazama

Commanding officer of the 101st Brigade's Independent Magic Battalion. Ranked lieutenant colonel.

Shigeru Sanada

Executive officer of the 101st Brigade's Independent Magic Battalion. Ranked major.

Kyouko Fujibayashi

Female officer serving as Kazama's aide. Ranked first lieutenant.

Hiromi Saeki

Commander of the Japan Ground Defense Force's 101st Brigade. Ranked major general. Superior officer to Harunobu Kazama, commanding officer of the Independent Magic Battalion. Due to her appearance, she is also known as the Silver Fox.

Muraji Yanagi

Executive officer of the 101st Brigade's Independent Magic Battalion. Ranked major.

Kousuke Yamanaka

Executive officer of the 101st Brigade's Independent Magic Battalion. Physician ranked major. First-rate healing magician.

Sakai

Belongs to the Japan Ground Defense Force's general headquarters. Ranked colonel. Seen as staunchly anti–Great Asian Alliance.

Gongjin Zhou

A handsome young man who brought Lu and Chen to Yokohama. A mysterious figure who hangs around Chinatown.

Xiangshan Chen

Leader of the Great Asian Alliance Army's Special Covert Forces. Has a heartless personality.

Ganghu Lu

The ace magician of the Great Asian Alliance Army's Special Covert Forces. Also known as the "Man-Eating Tiger."

Rin

A girl Morisaki saved. Her full name is Meiling Sun. The new leader of the Hong Kong–based international crime syndicate No-Head Dragon.

Miya Shiba
Tatsuya and Miyuki's actual mother. Deceased. The only magician skilled in mental construction interference magic.

Maya Yotsuba
Tatsuya and Miyuki's aunt. Miya's younger twin sister. The current head of the Yotsuba.

Honami Sakurai
Miya's Guardian. Deceased. Part of the first generation of the Sakura series, engineered magicians with strengthened magical capacity through genetic modification.

Hayama
An elderly butler employed by Maya.

Sayuri Shiba
Tatsuya and Miyuki's stepmother. Dislikes them.

Katsushige Shibata
Former candidate to become the next leader of the Yotsuba clan. Employed by the Ministry of Defense. An alum of Fifth High. Specializes in convergence magic.

Yuuka Tsukuba
Former candidate to become the next leader of the Yotsuba clan. Former vice president of First High's student council. Skilled at mental interference magic.

Kotona Tsutsumi
One of Katsushige Shibata's Guardians. A second-generation Bard series engineered magician. Specializes in sound-based magic.

Yoshimi
A Yotsuba magician related to the Kuroba. A psychometrist specializing in reading the psionic traces left behind in psionic information bodies. Very secretive.

Kanata Tsutsumi
One of Katsushige Shibata's Guardians. A second-generation Bard series engineered magician. Like his older sister, Kotona, he specializes in sound-based magic.

Angelina Kudou Shields

Commander of the USNA's magician unit, the Stars. Ranked major. Nickname is Lina. Also one of the strategic magicians called the Thirteen Apostles.

Virginia Balance

The USNA Joint Chiefs of Staff Information Bureau Internal Inspection Office's first deputy commissioner. Ranked colonel. Went to Japan in order to support Lina.

Silvia Mercury First

A planet-class magician in the USNA's magician unit, the Stars. Ranked warrant officer. Nickname is Silvie. Code name is Mercury First. During a mission in Japan, she serves as Major Sirius's aide.

Benjamin Canopus

Number two in the USNA's magician unit, the Stars. Ranked major. Takes command when Major Sirius is absent.

Mikaela Hongou

An agent sent into Japan by the USNA (although she actually works as a magic scientist for the Department of Defense). Nicknamed Mia.

Claire

Hunter Q—a female soldier in the magician unit Stardust for those who don't make it as Stars. Q refers to the 17th pursuit unit.

Alfred Fomalhaut

A first-degree star magician in the USNA's magician unit, the Stars. Rank is first lieutenant. Nicknamed Freddie. Currently AWOL.

Rachel

Hunter R—a female soldier in the magician unit Stardust for those who don't make it as Stars. R refers to the 18th pursuit unit.

Charles Sullivan

A satellite-class magician in the USNA's magician unit, the Stars. Code name is Deimos Second. Currently AWOL.

Kanda

A young politician affiliated with the Civil Rights Party. Supporter of civil rights in opposition to the military. Also anti-magician.

Raymond S. Clark

A student at the high school in Berkeley, USNA, where Shizuku studies abroad. A Caucasian boy who wastes no time making advances on Shizuku. Secretly one of the Seven Sages.

Kouzuke

A young Tokyo-based politician in the ruling party. Known as a legislator with favorable views toward magicians.

Igor Andreivich Bezobrazov

A strategic magician of the New Soviet Union and leading magic researcher at the Science Academy.

Mitsugu Kuroba

Miya Shiba and Maya Yotsuba's cousin. Father of Ayako and Fumiya.

Gu Jie

One of the Seven Sages. Also known as Gide Hague. A survivor of a Dahanese military's mage unit.

Ayako Kuroba

Tatsuya and Miyuki's second cousin. Has a younger twin brother named Fumiya. Student at Fourth High.

Joe Du

A mysterious man aiding Gu Jie's escape from Japan. Skilled enough at his job to consistently evade the Ten Master Clans magicians hunting them.

Fumiya Kuroba

Former candidate for the next head of the Yotsuba clan. Has an older twin sister named Ayako. Student at Fourth High.

Kazukiyo Oumi

Known as the Dollmaker, a magic researcher who specializes in necromancy and a practitioner of ancient magic. Rumored to use forbidden magic to reanimate corpses.

James Jackson

A tourist visiting Okinawa from Australia. Actually a—

Bradley Chan

A deserter of the Great Asian Alliance. Ranked first lieutenant.

Jasmine Jackson

James's daughter. She seems no older than twelve but acts mature for her age.

Daniel Liu

A deserter of the Great Asian Alliance, like Chan. Also one of the architects of the sabotage operation in Okinawa.

William MacLeod

A British strategic magician. A prodigy who has earned several teaching accolades from universities abroad.

Joseph Higaki

A military magician who fought the Great Asian Alliance alongside Tatsuya during the previous invasion of Okinawa. One of the Leftover Blood—descendants of orphaned children of the American soldiers who had been stationed in Okinawa.

Karla Schmidt

A German Union strategic magician and academic conducting research at Berlin University.

Mai Futatsugi

Head of the Futatsugi clan, one of the Ten Master Clans. Resides in Ashiya in Hyogo Prefecture. Publicly the majority shareholder in a variety of industrial chemical- and food-processing companies. Responsible for the Hanshin and Chugoku regions.

Kouichi Saegusa

Mayumi's father and current leader of the Saegusa clan. An ultra-top-class magician.

Saburou Nakura

A powerful magician employed by the Saegusa family. Mainly serves as Mayumi's personal bodyguard.

Gen Mitsuya

Head of the Mitsuya clan, one of the Ten Master Clans. Resides in Atsugi in Kanagawa Prefecture. While it isn't exactly public knowledge, he works as an international small arms broker. Manages Lab Three, which is still operational to this day.

Isami Itsuwa

Head of the Itsuwa clan, one of the Ten Master Clans. Resides in Uwajima in Ehime Prefecture. Publicly the executive and owner of a marine-shipping company. Responsible for the Tokai, Gifu, and Nagano regions.

Atsuko Mutsuzuka

Head of the Mutsuzuka clan, one of the Ten Master Clans. Resides in Sendai in Miyagi Prefecture. Publicly the owner of a geothermal energy exploration company. Responsible for the Tohoku region.

Raizou Yatsushiro

Head of the Yatsushiro clan, one of the Ten Master Clans. Resides in Fukuoka Prefecture. Publicly a university lecturer and majority shareholder in several telecommunications companies. Responsible for all of the Kyushu region, minus Okinawa.

Kazuki Juumonji

Former head of the Juumonji clan, one of the Ten Master Clans. Resides in Tokyo. Publicly the owner of a civil engineering and construction company that primarily serves the armed forces. Shares responsibility for the Kanto region, including Izu, with the Saegusa family.

Aoba Toudou

Yakumo refers to him as His Excellency, Priest Seiha. An old man with the shaved head of a priest, his origin and past are unknown. Per Yakumo, he appears to be a sponsor of the Yotsuba clan.

Tsukasa Tooyama

A member of the Tooyama clan, one of the Eighteen Support Clans, which aids the Ten Master Clans. The Tooyama exist to protect the functions of the state rather than the people.

Glossary

Course 1 student emblem

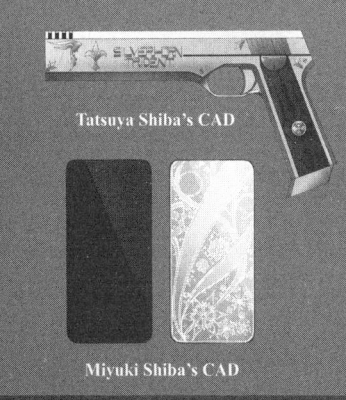

Tatsuya Shiba's CAD

Miyuki Shiba's CAD

Magic High School
Nickname for the high schools affiliated with the National Magic University. There are nine schools throughout the nation. First High to Third High adopt a system that splits its two hundred incoming freshmen into Course 1 and Course 2 students.

Blooms, Weeds
Slang terms used at First High to express the gap between Course 1 and Course 2 students. Course 1 student uniforms sport an eight-petaled emblem on the left breast, while Course 2 student uniforms do not.

CAD (Casting Assistant Device)
A device that simplifies magic casting. Magical programming is recorded within. There are many types and forms, some specialized and others multipurpose.

Four Leaves Technology (FLT)
A domestic CAD manufacturer. Originally more famous for magical-product engineering than for developing finished products, the development of the Silver model has made FLT much more widely known in their industry.

Taurus Silver
A genius engineer said to have advanced specialized CAD software by a decade in the span of a single year.

Eidos (individual information bodies)
Originally a term from Greek philosophy. In modern magic, eidos refers to the information bodies that accompany events. They form a so-called record of those events existing in the world, and can be considered the footprints of an object's state of being in the universe, be that active or passive. The definition of magic in its modern form is that of a technology that alters events by altering the information bodies composing them.

Idea (information body dimension)
Originally a term from Greek philosophy, pronounced "ee-dee-ah." In modern magic, Idea refers to the platform upon which eidos, or information bodies, are recorded. The primary function of magic is to yield a magic program (a spell sequence) on this Idea medium and overwrite the eidos recorded there.

Activation sequence
The blueprints of magic—and the programming that constructs it. Activation sequences are stored within CADs in a compressed format. Magicians send psionic waves into the CAD, which then expands the data and uses it to convert the activation sequence into a signal. This signal returns to the magician with the decompressed magic program.

Psions (thought particles)
Massless particles belonging to the dimension of spiritual phenomena. These information particles record products of awareness and thought. Eidos are considered the theoretical basis for modern magic, while activation sequences and magic programs are the technology forming its practical basis. All of three of these bodies of information are made of psions.

Pushions (spirit particles)
Massless particles belonging to the dimension of spiritual phenomena. Their existence has been confirmed, but their true form and function have yet to be determined. In general, magicians are only able to sense energized pushions.

Magician
An abbreviation of magic technician. This term refers to those with the skills to use magic at a practical level.

Magic program
An information body used to temporarily alter information connected to events. Constructed from psions possessed by magicians. Sometimes shortened to magigram.

Magic-calculation region

A mental region that constructs magic programs. The essential core of the talent of magic. Exists within the magician's unconscious regions. Though magicians can normally consciously use the magic-calculation region, they cannot perceive the processing happening within. The magic-calculation region may be called a black box, even for the magician performing the task.

Magic program output process

1. An activation sequence is transmitted to a CAD. This is called "reading an activation sequence."
2. Variables are added to the activation sequence and sent to the magic-calculation region.
3. A magic program is constructed from the activation sequence and its variables.
4. The constructed magic program is sent along the "route" from the highest part of the unconscious mind to the lowest part of the conscious mind, out the "gate" between consciousness and unconsciousness, and output to the Idea.
5. The magic program output interferes with the eidos at designated coordinates and overwrites them.

With a single-type, single-process spell, this five-stage process can be completed in under half a second. This is the bar for practical-level use with magicians.

Magic evaluation standards

The speed with which a magician constructs psionic information bodies is known as magical throughput, or processing speed. The scale and scope of the information bodies magicians can construct is known as magical capacity. The strength with which magicians overwrite eidos with magic programs is known as magical power.

Cardinal Code hypothesis

A school of thought claiming there is the existence of a total of sixteen foundational plus and minus magic programs within the eight types of magic—acceleration, weighting, movement, vibration, convergence, dispersion, absorption, and emission.

Typed magic

Any magic belonging to the four families and eight types.

Exotyped magic

A term for spells that control mental phenomena rather than physical ones. Encompasses many fields, from divine magic and spirit magic—which employs spiritual presences—to mind reading, astral form separation, and consciousness control.

Ten Master Clans

The most powerful magician organization in Japan. The ten families are chosen every four years from among the following twenty-eight families: Ichijou, Ichinokura, Isshiki, Futatsugi, Nikaidou, Nihei, Mitsuya, Mikazuki, Yotsuba, Itsuwa, Gotou, Itsumi, Mutsuzuka, Rokkaku, Rokugou, Roppongi, Saegusa, Shippou, Tanabata, Nanase, Yatsushiro, Hassaku, Hachiman, Kudou, Kuki, Kuzumi, Juumonji, and Tooyama.

Numbers

Just like how the Ten Master Clans contain a number from one to ten in their surnames, well-known families within the Hundred Families use numbers eleven or greater, such as Chiyoda (one thousand), Isori (fifty), and Chiba (one thousand). Although the number value is not equivalent to the family's level of strength, the presence of a number in a surname is a broad indication of that family's prominent lineage and talent.

Non-numbers

Also called Extra Numbers, or simply Extras. Magician families who have been stripped of their number. Back in the day when magicians were used as weapons and experimental subjects, success cases were given numbers, while failures—those who did not produce sufficient results—were not.

Various Spells

• Cocytus
Exotyped magic that freezes the mind. A frozen mind cannot order the flesh to die, so anyone subject to this spell enters a state of mental and physical stasis.

• Rumbling
An old spell that vibrates the ground to create a medium for an independent information body known as a spirit.

• Program Dispersion
A spell that dismantles a magic program, the main component of a spell, into a group of psionic particles with no meaningful structure. Since magic programs affect the information bodies associated with events, it is necessary for the information structure to be exposed, leaving no way to prevent interference against the magic program itself.

• Program Demolition
A typeless spell that rams a mass of compressed psionic particles directly into an object without passing through the Idea, causing it to explode and blow away the psionic information bodies recorded in magic, such as activation sequences and magic programs. Although this spell is considered a type of magic because it is a psionic bullet without any structure such as a magic program for altering events, it is not affected by Information Boost or Area Interference. The pressure of the bullet itself also repels any Cast Jamming effects. Since it has zero physical effect, it is unblockable.

• Mine Origin
A spell that imparts strong vibrations to anything that can be conceptualized as the ground—including dirt, boulders, sand, and concrete—regardless of its composition.

• Fissure
A spell that uses independent information bodies or spirits as a medium to push a line into the ground and create a fissure in the earth.

• Dry Blizzard
A spell that gathers carbon dioxide from the air, creates dry-ice particles, then converts the extra heat energy from the freezing process to kinetic energy to launch the dry-ice particles at a high speed.

• Slithering Thunders
In addition to condensing the water vapor from Dry Blizzard's dry-ice evaporation and creating a highly conductive mist with the evaporated carbon dioxide in it, this spell creates static electricity with vibration-type magic and emission-type magic. A combination spell, it also fires an electric attack at an enemy using the carbon gas–filled mist and water droplets as a conductor.

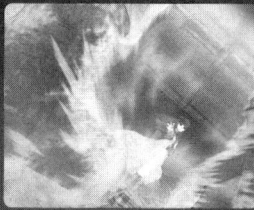

• Niflheim
A vibration- and deceleration-type area-of-effect spell. It chills a large volume of air, then moves it to freeze a wide range. In blunt terms, it creates a super-large refrigerator. The white mist that appears upon activation is the particles of frozen ice and dry ice, but at higher levels, a mist of frozen liquid nitrogen occurs.

• Burst
A dispersion-type spell that vaporizes the liquid inside a target object. When used on a creature, the spell will vaporize bodily fluids and cause the body to rupture. When used on a machine powered by internal combustion, the spell vaporizes the fuel and makes it explode. Fuel cells see the same result, and even if no combustible fuel is on board, there is no machine that does not contain some liquid, such as battery fluid, hydraulic fluid, coolant, or lubricant; once Burst activates, virtually any machine will be destroyed.

• Disheveled Hair
An old spell that, instead of specifying a direction and changing the wind's direction to that, uses air current control to bring about the vague result of "tangling" it, causing currents along the ground that entangle an opponent's feet in the grass. Only usable on plains with grass of a certain height.

Magic Swords

Aside from fighting techniques that use magic itself as a weapon, another method of magical combat involves techniques for using magic to strengthen and control weapons. The majority of these spells combine magic with projectile weapons such as guns and bows, but the art of the sword, known as kenjutsu, has developed in Japan as well as a way to link magic with sword techniques. This has led to magic technicians formulating personal-use magic techniques known as magic swords, which can be said to be both modern and ancient magic.

1. High-Frequency Blade

A spell that locally liquefies a solid body and cleaves it by causing a blade to vibrate at a high speed, then propagate the vibration that exceeds the molecular cohesive force of matter it comes in contact with. Used as a set with a spell to prevent the blade from breaking.

2. Pressure Cut

A spell that generates left-right perpendicular repulsive force relative to the angle of a slashing blade edge, causing the blade to force apart any object it touches and thereby cleave it. The size of the repulsive field is less than a millimeter, but it has the strength to interfere with light, so when seen from the front, the blade edge becomes a black line.

3. Douji-Giri (Simultaneous Cut)

An ancient magic spell passed down as a secret sword art of the Genji. It is a magic sword technique wherein the user remotely manipulates two blades through a third in their hands in order to have the swords surround an opponent and slash simultaneously. *Douji* is the Japanese pronunciation for both "simultaneous" and "child," so this ambiguity was used to keep the inherited nature of the technique a secret.

4. Zantetsu (Iron Cleaver)

A secret sword art of the Chiba clan. Rather than defining a katana as a hulk of steel and iron, this movement spell defines it as a single concept, then the spell moves the katana along a slashing path set by the magic program. The result is that the katana is defined as a mono-molecular blade, never breaking, bending, or chipping as it slices through any objects in its path.

5. Jinrai Zantetsu (Lightning Iron Cleaver)

An expanded version of Zantetsu that makes use of the Ikazuchi-Maru, a personal-armament device. By defining the katana and its wielder as one collective concept, the spell executes the entire series of actions, from enemy contact to slash, incredibly quickly and with faultless precision.

6. Mountain Tsunami

A secret sword art of the Chiba clan that makes use of the Orochi-Maru, a giant personal weapon that is six feet long. The user minimizes their own inertia and that of their katana while approaching an enemy at a high speed and, at the moment of impact, adds the neutralized inertia to the blade's inertia and slams the target with it. The longer the approach run, the greater the false inertial mass, reaching a maximum of ten tons.

7. Usuba Kagerou (Antlion)

A spell that uses hardening magic to anchor a five-nanometer-thick sheet of woven carbon nanotube to a perfect surface and make it a blade. The blade that Usuba Kagerou creates is sharper than any sword or razor, but the spell contains no functions to support moving the blade, demanding technical sword skill and ability from the user.

Magic Technician Development Institutes

Laboratories for the purpose of magician development that the Japanese government established one after another in response to the geopolitical climate, which had become strained prior to World War III in the 2030s. Their objectives were not to develop magic but specifically to develop magicians, researching various methods to give birth to human specimens who were most suitable for areas of magic that were considered important, including, but not limited to, genetic engineering.

Ten magic technician development institutes were established, numbered as such, and even today, five are still in operation.

The details of each institute's research are described below.

Magic Technician Development Institute One

Established in Kanazawa in 2031. Currently shut down.

Its research focus, revolving around close combat, was the development of magic that directly manipulated biological organisms. The vaporization spell Burst is derived from this facility's research. Notably, magic that could control a human body's movements was forbidden as it enabled puppet terrorism (suicide attacks using victims that had been turned into puppets).

Magic Technician Development Institute Two

Established on Awaji Island in 2031. Currently in operation. Develops magic opposite to that of Lab One, e.g. magic that can manipulate inorganic objects, especially absorption-type spells related to oxidation-reduction reactions.

Magic Technician Development Institute Three

Established in Atsugi in 2032. Currently in operation.

With its goal of developing magicians who can react to a variety of situations when operating independently, this facility is the main driver behind the research on multicasting. In particular, it tests the limits of how many spells are possible during simultaneous casting and continual casting and develops magicians who can simultaneously cast multiple spells.

Magic Technician Development Institute Four

Details unknown. Its location is speculated to be near the old prefectural border between Tokyo and Yamanashi. Its establishment is believed to have occurred in 2033. It is assumed to be shut down, but the truth of that matter is unknown. Lab Four is rumored to be the only magic research facility that was established not only with government support but also investment from private sponsors who held strong influence over the nation; it is currently operating without government oversight and being managed directly by those sponsors. Rumors also say that those sponsors actually took over control of the facility before the 2020s.

It is said that its goal is to use mental interference magic to strengthen the very wellspring of the talent called magic, which exists in a magician's unconscious—the magic calculation region itself.

Magic Technician Development Institute Five

Established in Uwajima, Shikoku, in 2035. Currently in operation.

Researches magic that can manipulate various forms of matter. Its main focus, fluid control, is not technically difficult, but it has also succeeded in manipulating various solid forms. The fruits of its research include Bahamut, a spell jointly developed with the USNA. Along with the fluid-manipulation spell Abyss, it is known internationally as a magic research facility that developed two strategic-class spells.

Magic Technician Development Institute Six

Established in Sendai in 2035. Currently in operation. Researches magical heat control. Along with Lab Eight, it gives the impression of being a facility more for basic research than military purposes. However, it is said that they conducted the most genetic manipulation experiments out of all the magic technician development institutes, aside from Lab Four. (Though, of course, the full account of Lab Four's situation is not possible.)

Magic Technician Development Institute Seven

Established in Tokyo in 2036. Currently shut down.

Developed magic with an emphasis on anti-group combat. It successfully created colony control magic. Contrary to Lab Six, which was largely a nonmilitary organization, Lab Seven was established as a magician development research facility that could be relied on for assistance in defending the capital in case of an emergency.

Magic Technician Development Institute Eight

Established in Kitakyushu in 2037. Currently in operation.

Researches magical control of gravitational force, electromagnetic force, strong force, and weak force. It is a pure research institute to a greater extent than even Lab Six. However, unlike Lab Six, its relationship to the JDF is steadfast. This is because Lab Eight's research focus can be easily linked to nuclear weapons development, (though they currently avoid such connotations thanks to the JDF's seal of approval).

Magic Technician Development Institute Nine

Established in Nara in 2037. Currently shut down. This facility tried to solve several problems modern magic struggled with, such as fuzzy spell manipulation, through a fusion of modern and old magic, integrating ancient knowledge into modern techniques.

Magic Technician Development Institute Ten

Established in Tokyo in 2039. Currently shut down. Like Lab Seven, doubled as capital defense, researching area magic that could create virtual structures in space as a means of defending against high-firepower attacks. It resulted in a myriad of anti-physical barrier spells.

Lab Ten also aimed to raise magic abilities through different means from Lab Four. More specifically, rather than enhancing the magic calculation region itself, they grappled with developing magicians who responded as needed by temporarily overclocking their magic calculation regions to use powerful magic. Whether their research was successful has not been made public.

Aside from these ten institutes, other laboratories with the goal of developing Elements were operational from the 2010s to the 2020s, but they are currently all shut down. In addition, the JDF possesses a secret research facility directly under the Ground Defense Force's General Headquarters' jurisdiction, established in 2002, which is still carrying on its research. Retsu Kudou underwent enhancement operations at this institution before moving to Lab Nine.

Strategic Magicians: The Thirteen Apostles

Because modern magic was born into a highly technological world, only a few nations were able to develop strong magic for military purposes. As a result, only a handful were able to develop "strategic-class magic," which rivaled weapons of mass destruction.

However, these nations shared the magic they developed with their allies, and certain magicians of allied nations with high aptitudes for strategic-class magic came to be known as strategic magicians.

As of April 2095, there are thirteen magicians publicly recognized as strategic-class magicians by their nations. They are called the Thirteen Apostles and are considered important players in the world's military balance. The Thirteen Apostles' nations, names and strategic spell names are listed below.

USNA

Angie Sirius: Heavy Metal Burst
Elliott Miller: Leviathan
Laurent Barthes: Leviathan
* The only apostle belonging to the Stars is Angie Sirius. Elliott Miller is stationed at Alaska Base, and Laurent Barthes is stationed outside the country at Gibraltar Base. For the most part, their positions don't change.

New Soviet Union

Igor Andreivich Bezobrazov: Tuman Bomba
Leonid Kondratenko: Zemlja Armija
* As Kondratenko is of advanced age, he generally stays at the Black Sea base.

Great Asian Alliance

Yunde Liu: Pilita (Thunderclap Tower)
*Yunde Liu died on October 31, 2095, in the battle against Japan.

Indo-Persian Federation

Barat Chandra Khan: Agni Downburst

Japan

Mio Itsuwa: Abyss

Brazil

Miguel Diez: Synchroliner Fusion
* This magic program was named by the USNA.

England

William MacLeod: Ozone Circle

Germany

Karla Schmidt: Ozone Circle
* Ozone Circle is based on a spell codeveloped by nations in the EU before its split as a means to fix the hole in the ozone layer. The magic program was perfected by England and then publicized to the old EU through a convention.

Turkey

Ali Sahin: Bahamut
* This magic program was developed in cooperation with the USNA and Japan, then provided to Turkey by Japan.

Thailand

Somchai Bunnag: Agni Downburst
* This magic program was provided by Indo-Persia.

The International Situation
State of the World in 2096

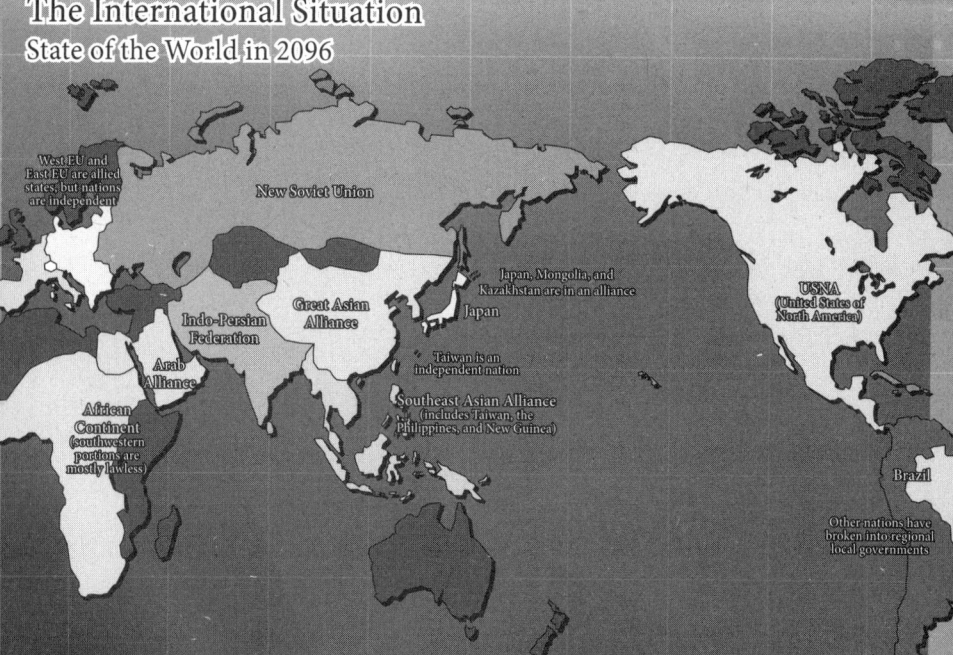

World War III, also called the Twenty Years' Global War Outbreak, was directly triggered by global cooling, and it fundamentally redrew the world map.

The USA annexed Canada and the countries from Mexico to Panama to form the United States of North America, or the USNA.

Russia reabsorbed Ukraine and Belarus to form the New Soviet Union.

China conquered northern Burma, northern Vietnam, northern Laos, and the Korean Peninsula to form the Great Asian Alliance, or GAA.

India and Iran absorbed several central Asian countries (Turkmenistan, Uzbekistan, Tajikistan, and Afghanistan) and South Asian countries (Pakistan, Nepal, Bhutan, Bangladesh, and Sri Lanka) to form the Indo-Persian Federation.

The other Asian and Arab countries formed regional military alliances to resist the three superpowers: the New Soviet Union, GAA, and the Indo-Persian Federation.

Australia chose national isolation.

The EU failed to unify and split into an eastern and a western section along the border between Germany and France. These east-west groupings also failed to properly form unions and now are actually weaker than they were before unification.

Africa saw half its nations destroyed altogether, with the surviving ones barely managing to retain urban control.

South America, excluding Brazil, fell into small, isolated states administered on a local government level.

[1]

April 14, 2097. At Yokohama's Kanto Branch of the Magic Association, the Youth Council ended before noon as planned. Unfortunately, no progress was made. Tatsuya left the council room as soon as the meeting ended. Just then, a voice called out to him.

"Mr. Yotsuba, wait!"

Tatsuya spun around. He wasn't a Yotsuba, but he couldn't ignore someone just because they got his name wrong. That would be childish. Then again, he wasn't above flouting Ten Master Clan conventions when the mood struck him.

"Saegusa," he replied, dropping all formalities. "How can I help you?"

"Lunch is going to be served for all of the Youth Council attendees," Saegusa said, his voice and expression betraying his impatience. "Won't you join us?"

Tatsuya knew about the lunch, of course, which was why he announced his plans before leaving the council room.

"Sorry," he said firmly. "As I said before, I have urgent business to take care of."

"We promise not to take too much of your time," Saegusa pressed.

"Again, I appreciate the invitation, but I really have to go."

Tatsuya understood how Tomokazu felt, but he had his own matters to deal with. It was nothing personal.

"I'll see you later," he said with a curt bow.

"Mr. Shiba," another voice called out. This time, it was a young woman.

"Yes?" Tatsuya turned to find a Magic Association employee. She hesitated for a moment in front of Tomokazu but quickly got down to business.

"A VTOL has arrived for you on the rooftop," she stated flatly.

"Ah. All right."

No one had told him he was getting picked up, but he figured it would be quicker to check out in person than ask questions. Tatsuya gave Tomokazu another parting bow before following the Magic Association employee to the building's rooftop.

Once there, he found a compact VTOL with tilt-rotors fixed to the main wings. It looked like it could fit about six people, minus the pilot. A young man in a double-breasted suit standing beside the aircraft bowed to Tatsuya as he approached.

He motioned to the aircraft door: "After you, Master Tatsuya."

Each of the young man's words and gestures oozed with politeness. Judging by the VIP treatment, Tatsuya figured he worked for the Yotsuba clan. Although this was undoubtedly the first time they had met, the young man felt strangely familiar.

"Nice to meet you," Tatsuya greeted. "You probably already know this, but I'm Tatsuya Shiba."

"Oh! Beg your pardon. I should have introduced myself sooner," the young man apologized with an over-the-top bow. "My name is Hyougo Hanabishi. It's a pleasure to make your acquaintance."

Tatsuya put two and two together. That's why the young man seemed so familiar—he was Hanabishi's son.

Hanabishi was the Yotsuba clan's second butler after Hayama, and he was in charge of organizing both personnel and equipment for covert combat operations. Tatsuya had heard his eldest son was working under an alias in a private military and security company (PMSC) in the UK to get experience in the field. Apparently, he had already returned home.

"I've been entrusted with the important task of accompanying you and Lady Miyuki to the main house today," Hyougo explained and motioned again to the aircraft door. "Please. After you."

"Understood, thanks." Tatsuya unlocked the back door of the VTOL with the electronic key the Yotsuba clan had provided him and climbed into the aircraft. This was a typical identification procedure. He didn't feel strange about unlocking the aircraft door himself. Likewise, Hyougo Hanabishi maintained a placid expression as he gently shut the door behind his passenger.

Hyougo landed the VTOL on the rooftop helipad of a newly built ten-story high-rise in Chofu. The first three floors were dedicated to office space, and floors four to ten were residential. Tatsuya didn't recognize the building, and it was clearly not their final destination.

Immediately after the aircraft's rotors settled, three figures emerged from the penthouse—two young girls and one woman in her thirties. Since the VTOL was electric, Tatsuya initially thought they were stopping to recharge its batteries. He quickly realized he was mistaken. He opened the aircraft door and helped the taller girl inside.

"Thank you, Tatsuya." She smiled.

The two girls were Miyuki and Minami. The original plan had been for them to wait at home, but the main house must have picked them up and brought them to this location.

"Of course," Tatsuya replied. "Did you two wait long?"

"Only about fifteen minutes," Miyuki said. "The waiting room was quite comfortable."

It all made sense now. This penthouse was probably meant to be a rest stop for helipad users.

"Good," he said.

"Hello, Tatsuya," Minami greeted.

Tatsuya acknowledged her with a nod and made sure both girls were safely inside the VTOL. Then he locked the door and signaled to the young pilot.

"Whenever you're ready, Hanabishi."

"Yes, sir."

Minami's eyes went wide with surprise. Like Tatsuya, this was her first time seeing Hyougo in person. Hyougo, meanwhile, was unfazed by Minami's shock. He had been met with this kind of reaction countless times since coming home and was mostly used to it. Without providing any sort of introduction to his new passengers, he started up the VTOL and took off.

The compact VTOL carrying Tatsuya and his two companions didn't land directly in the hidden village where the Yotsuba clan resided. Instead, it stopped at the foot of a mountain near Kobuchizawa Station.

"This way," Hyougo said, leading his passengers off the helipad to an air traffic control building.

Tatsuya figured they would be transferring to a car to complete their journey to the main house. His prediction wasn't wrong, but the route they took came as a surprise.

Instead of exiting the air control building, Hyougo led them into an employee-only elevator.

His guests gave him quizzical looks as he opened an emergency control panel with an old-fashioned dimple key. Almost simultaneously, the elevator doors closed. Hyougo tipped a palm print recognition panel toward himself and placed his right hand on the screen. In under a second, the elevator cage carrying the group began its descent.

"We're going down pretty far…," Miyuki said to Tatsuya with a hint of uneasiness.

Hyougo replied, "Our destination lies eighty meters underground."

Just as he finished speaking, the elevator began to slow down. Soon enough, its cage came to a complete stop, and the doors slid open.

The party exited the elevator into a hall that led to a spacious porte cochere. Beyond it was a shortcut illuminated by artificial light.

A large luxury sedan waited for them there. As far as Tatsuya could tell, the vehicle looked completely empty.

Hyougo opened a back seat door for Miyuki and Tatsuya, in turn. Then he took a seat at the wheel. Once Minami was settled in the passenger seat, he started up the car.

"This underground road leads directly to the main house," Hyougo explained. "Sadly, it doesn't offer much of a view, but I promise it will not be a long ride."

Under the monotonous illumination of countless light panels, the large black sedan zipped down the path at a speed considered illegal on public roads. As Hyougo assured them, it took less than ten minutes to reach the main house.

The Chiba family's main dojo was located near the border between Tokyo and Kawasaki Prefecture. The dojo itself tended to be livelier on Sundays since most of its pupils were company employees, and this was their day off.

On weekdays, there were no school-age kids during the daytime. The fact that Erika, a student at magic high school, was around at this time of day could only mean it was the weekend.

Ever since Toshikazu, the clan head's eldest son, passed away, a tragic darkness had fallen over the dojo. Not even Erika's upbeat presence could lift the persistent gloom. But whenever she showed up for practice, she did have a knack for helping everyone feel more positive and productive. The two boys she brought along with her on this day also helped lighten the mood in their own way.

"Yah!"

"Ugh!"

There was a loud thump as a violent tremor traveled across the floor. Everyone in the dojo looked up with perturbed curiosity to search for the source of the noise. The culprit was a long-haired boy now lying on his back and groaning. In front of him, a large, burly boy exhaled loudly.

"Ready for a break, Saburou?" the larger boy asked.

"Not yet!"

Saburou jumped to his feet. While unsteady at first, he quickly steadied his stance, looking almost like he hadn't taken any damage at all.

He bowed to his opponent at an almost perfect 90-degree angle and shouted, "One more round, Saijou!"

"Hah!" Leo scoffed, turning to Erika. "What do you say, Erika? Do I have your permission to continue?"

"Sure," she said, holding Saburou's solemn gaze. "In fact, you can keep going until one of you can't stand."

A smirk crossed Leo's mouth. "You really think that'll happen to me?"

"I never said that." Erika shook her head. "In fact, I won't let you live it down if you let an underclassman beat you."

She looked dead serious, but Leo just shrugged. "Yes, ma'am."

He spun back to his opponent, gripping his bamboo sword in one hand. Saburou quickly followed suit.

Both boys assumed the same one-handed stance, but there was a dramatic difference. Leo's weapon was classified as an *odachi*, which was longer than the standard sword. Saburou's weapon, on the other hand, was the length of a *wakizashi*, making it notably shorter.

The length of a fighter's sword didn't provide any absolute advantages or disadvantages, but it did mean each one lent itself to a particular fighting style. Generally, weapons with a longer reach were better suited to making the first move; shorter swords were more appropriate for avoiding or parrying an opponent's attack and bringing the fight into close range.

This time, however—after a brief standoff—it was Saburou who made the first move. He shifted forward, but Leo wasn't about to let the younger boy have his way. The moment Saburou entered his reach, Leo quickly swung his weapon, further extending the distance between the two. Saburou couldn't parry the blow.

It wasn't just fast; it was also more powerful than any ordinary fighter's two-handed swing. It took Saburou everything he had to evade the attack while keeping both hands on the grip of his *wakizashi*.

Now it was a battle between one- and two-handed stances. Even though Saburou evaded his attack, Leo's stance didn't falter. In fact, it was Saburou—driven back by his opponent's sword—who was showing obvious signs of exertion.

Despite the considerable length and weight of his bamboo sword, Leo once again swung it savagely with ease. This time, Saburou was caught off balance.

Suddenly, a small mock sword shot out from the sheath at his waist. He didn't throw it; the small blade slipped out on its own. It flew through the air and headed straight for Leo's face.

Leo stopped midswing and swatted the small sheath sword away with the pommel of his blade. But the small weapon—which was slimmer than a dagger and essentially a needle compared to Leo's larger sword—didn't fall to the floor. To Leo's horror, it split into two shards that sailed toward either side of his head. His face tensed.

Rather than intercepting the small sword, he boldly pressed forward. Now the distance between the two boys was too small for Leo's big sword. Even if he swung with good form, he wouldn't be able to follow through properly. But this wasn't an official kendo match, and bamboo swords weren't real swords. There was no obligation to follow the standard rules.

Leo wrapped his left hand around the middle of his bamboo sword's blade and thrust it forward like a spear. Saburou tumbled across the mats to avoid the blow.

Meanwhile, the two pieces of Saburou's small sheath sword

plummeted to the floor like a lifeless puppet. The younger boy's evasion was an attempt to move away and widen the distance between him and his opponent.

At the same time, this made it perfect for a different move. A wildness flashed through Leo's eyes—he wasn't about to miss this chance.

"Hrrrahhh!" he yelled, bringing down his sword.

Knowing he couldn't avoid the blow, Saburou tried to intercept the long blade at the last second. Balancing on one knee, he held both ends of the short sword above his head. The adrenaline made him feel like his bamboo sword was a real weapon. Leo's large *odachi* slammed into the middle of Saburou's blade, sending the younger boy tumbling to his back. Although he had succeeded in catching the blow, both blades had crashed into his forehead, and it clearly hit him hard.

Leo turned to Erika with a panicked look on his face. But Erika's gaze was focused on Saburou.

"Give him first aid," she said to one of the observers.

"Right away, Miss Erika."

A man in his thirties jogged over to Saburou, knelt by the boy's head, and fiddled with his CAD. After a few seconds, he placed his hands over Saburou's forehead and began casting healing magic.

The redness on Saburou's forehead receded instantly. Healing magic was a technique that tricked the world into believing that the body was uninjured. The results were immediately apparent. It didn't take the universe long to realize that this was pure fabrication. Before the effect of the lie wore off, a new lie had to be created. In other words, healing magic essentially was a stopgap that pretended an injury was cured until it was truly healed. As a result, the injured person could fight in virtually perfect condition as long as the healing spell remained in effect.

Saburou quickly regained consciousness and sprang to his feet. He was clearly ready to jump back into the fight. But Erika intervened.

"Stop," she said firmly. "That's enough for today. Any more and you'll have to deal with real physical consequences."

Saburou stood down. "...Fine."

Although not blessed with the magic required to serve as a clan bodyguard, Saburou had a strong understanding of magic thanks to his association with the Mitsuya clan and was familiar with the limits of healing magic.

He lowered his head in Leo's direction. "Thank you for your time." Then he bowed to Erika and started to walk away.

"Wait," Erika called out. "Why are you leaving? We're not done yet."

Saburou froze, his feet glued to the mats. It was as if Erika had read his mind. She pushed down on the crown of his head, forcing him to sit. He stepped back a few paces and knelt next to the wall so as not to be in anyone's way. Erika knelt down directly in front of him, and Leo took a cross-legged position at her side.

"Yaguruma would have won with that last attack if he hadn't stopped actively using his psychokinesis," Erika began.

"Timing-wise, it would've been a draw," Leo rebutted.

"Timing-wise, yes," she replied diplomatically. "But you have to admit, Yaguruma responded to *all* of your strikes. You, on the other hand, were completely thrown off guard when his small sheath sword flew at your face. Admit it. You lost this one."

Leo didn't argue, but he clearly wasn't convinced, either. Erika ignored his frustration and turned her attention to Saburou.

"You seem to think poorly of your psychokinetic abilities because you can't move heavy objects. But even a small, 100-gram blade can be lethal if it hits someone's vitals. PK isn't only a means of restraint; it's also a *weapon* that can eliminate an enemy. It's important to understand that."

"No, I do understand," Saburou shot back. But even Leo could tell this was a reflexive response that lacked confidence. Erika, too, was not one to be fooled.

"Then forget about understanding," she said. "Have confidence in your own strength."

Saburou gritted his teeth in frustration. There had been a time when he was confident in his strength. In himself. All the training he went through was a sign of this confidence in his abilities to become Shiina's shield.

Unfortunately, the harsh reality was that he wasn't strong enough. His strength had betrayed him once before, and it was no easy task to rebuild that confidence.

The Yotsuba clan's main house was approximately an hour away from Yokohama's Kanto Branch of the Magic Association. However, Tatsuya's group arrived in half that time.

Hayama was quick to greet the party as they stepped out of the car.

"Master Tatsuya. Lady Miyuki," he said warmly. "The lady of the house awaits. Please follow me."

Hayama was the head of the Yotsuba clan's servants and Maya's right-hand man. The politeness he showed toward Miyuki and Tatsuya proved that their respective positions as heiress and her fiancé were more than just a title.

Miyuki followed directly behind Hayama, followed by Minami, Tatsuya, and Hyougo at the rear. Minami was one thing. Tatsuya was mainly surprised by Hayama's lack of acknowledgment of Hyougo.

Is he just the driver in charge of picking us up? Tatsuya wondered. But he lost his chance to ask. Before they knew it, the party found themselves in the main house's cafeteria. This was the same place where Miyuki was nominated the temporary head after gathering a group of candidates at the end of the year.

Katsushige Shibata, Yuuka Tsukuba, the fraternal twins Fumiya Kuroba and Ayako Kuroba—these were the members present on that fated New Year's Eve. And they were there on this day, too. The only difference was, unlike last time, Maya had joined them.

"Sorry to keep you waiting," Tatsuya apologized.

"Nonsense," Maya replied generously. "You're not even late. Please. Take a seat."

"Thank you." Tatsuya bowed, and Miyuki followed suit.

Tatsuya then turned to offer Miyuki a chair, but Minami was already ahead of him. Recognizing his good intentions, Miyuki gratefully met his gaze before taking a seat.

Meanwhile, Hyougo offered Tatsuya a seat.

It's almost as if the Yotsuba clan is planning to assign him as my personal servant, the young Shiba mused.

Once everyone was seated, Hayama rang a small bell. Before its brass echoes faded, a maid scurried in, pushing a wagon. It was as if she had been standing by this whole time, waiting for the signal.

While it was too late for lunch, Maya must have guessed that her guests would come straight to the main house without eating. A light meal with tea was laid out in front of the two Shiba siblings.

Tatsuya realized Minami had not had lunch, either. He felt bad about making her stand behind Miyuki with an empty stomach. At the same time, he knew it would be an insult to offer her some tea when she was on duty. With this in mind, he decided to remain silent and—with Maya's permission—started to eat. Miyuki followed her brother's lead.

Of course, neither Tatsuya nor Miyuki was rude enough to focus solely on eating. They made sure to respond to Maya, Yuuka, and Ayako's small talk between bites of food and sips of tea. Once they finished their leisurely meal, Maya's expression changed. Tatsuya and Miyuki sat upright in their chairs, anticipating what was coming.

"Well, then," the Yotsuba clan head began. "Let's have our first point of business be Saika New Island."

"Of course," Tatsuya responded promptly. He proceeded to explain the events that took place on the main island of Okinawa, Kumejima Island, the artificial island, and other offshore areas in a sequential and brief fashion.

"As for the Australian agents, Captain James J. Johnson and Captain Jasmine Williams," he continued, "it seems they were transferred to Miyaki Island."

"Yes, I've been informed," Maya said. "Thank you for your hard work in that area."

Miyaki Island was a small landmass fifty kilometers east of Miyake Island that was newly formed due to rapid volcanic activity in 2001, the Year of the Snake. It was also called the New 21st Century Island, since it was formed in the first year of the twenty-first century.

The island was originally used as a base for the National Defense Force during the Twenty Years' Global War Outbreak. However, due to repeated eruptions in the 2050s, the base was abandoned. It was now used as a facility for incarcerating dangerous magicians.

In fact, through Aoba Toudou's sponsorship, the Yotsuba clan now privately owned Miyaki Island. On paper, the island was owned by a real estate company in Tokyo, but the Yotsuba clan controlled all of the real estate company's shares. In essence, the Yotsuba owned everything the company owned.

The National Defense Force entrusted the Yotsuba clan to use Miyaki Island as a place to isolate criminals. That meant that Maya had unrestricted access to all the data on prisoners sent there. Tatsuya explicitly mentioned Johnson and Jasmine because he knew his aunt could confirm his suspicions about where they had been placed.

"Weren't there plans to turn Miyaki into a research facility for experiments?" Katsushige Shibata asked suspiciously. Ever since it was decided that Miyuki would take over the position as head of the main family and Katsushige would take over a branch, he had been involved in family business while working for the Ministry of Defense. That meant he was familiar with the projects the Yotsuba family was working on.

"Oh, don't worry about that. We were going to dispose of it anyway," Maya said.

Katsushige's brow furrowed slightly at this response. But that was the extent of the reactions at the table. Despite Maya's ambiguous wording, it was clear to everyone in the room what was going to be disposed of. They either chose to let it pass without comment or simply didn't react at all. Ayako was one of the latter.

"Isn't Miyaki Island where Miyuki practiced Niflheim?" she asked. "Will we be continuing this tradition by turning the research facility you're planning into a large, outdoor lab?"

From the nature of her questions, it was clear that Ayako was mostly interested in the new facility rather than the island itself. It was true that Miyuki used it as a practice ground in middle school to master Niflheim.

The prison for dangerous magicians was established afterward. However, only a small part of the west end of the island was dedicated to the prison. Due to recurring undersea volcanic activity, the island was largely composed of lava bed, measuring eight square kilometers—roughly the same size as Tokyo's Kunitachi City. There was plenty of room to practice large-scale cooling magic.

"Nothing is confirmed yet, but..." Maya paused. She wasn't playing coy; she seemed genuinely conflicted whether to continue her sentence. "Hmm... I guess I can tell you." She took a breath and began. "You know how our facilities have been falling apart with age."

Everyone in the room nodded. Most of Yotsuba clan's facilities were inherited from Lab Four and dated back to the war. Although repairs and renovations were made as needed, the buildings' fundamental design was increasingly dated.

"I am not implying we should tear down our existing equipment and replace it with something totally new," Maya continued. "That could spark its own set of issues."

This time, only Tatsuya and Katsushige nodded. Many of the facilities from the war were difficult to rebuild. A complete renovation project could mean completely halting research in several areas.

"Instead, I decided to build a brand-new facility on Miyaki Island," Maya concluded.

"Do you have the National Defense Force's approval to abolish the prisons we've been managing?" Yuuka prompted. Unlike Katsushige, this was the first time she was hearing about the project.

"There is no need to worry about that," Maya replied calmly. "We will continue to run the current prisons on the surface. Besides, the new facility we are building is a National Defense Force research lab in name."

"But won't there be a problem with us taking control of a facility like that?" Yuuka persisted.

"It has already been taken care of," Maya said firmly.

Clearly having no intention to discuss the details, she shifted her gaze to Tatsuya and continued, "But enough about that. I am much more interested in hearing the rest of Tatsuya's report. That spell you invented to nullify a magician's magic—Gatekeeper, was it? Is it possible for other magicians to use it?"

"I'll have to tinker with the sequence more," Tatsuya replied, "but anyone proficient in mental interference magic should theoretically be able to."

Yuuka and Fumiya suddenly seemed interested. These two were some of the most adept magicians at mental interference–type magic in the Yotsuba clan. While not technically up to par with their parents yet, they were still in the running for best or second best in the family.

"Have you put it into code yet?" Maya asked.

"Yes." Tatsuya nodded. "I've brought it with me, actually."

To put a spell into code meant to transcribe it into an activation sequence. Magicians mostly created new spells intuitively. Writing those spells as activation sequences required specialized skills and was currently a fundamental obstacle to sharing magic.

Tatsuya, however, developed new spells from activation sequences already, so he had no difficulty putting spells into code. Knowing this and assuming he had already created the activation sequence, Maya urged him to present his results.

"Good," Maya said. "Give it to Hayama."

"Yes, ma'am."

She turned to Yuuka. "Get a copy of the activation sequence from Hayama once he has them."

"Will do," Yuuka replied.

Then back to Tatsuya: "I am considering putting the Tsukaba family in charge of improving Gatekeeper. What do you think?"

"Yes, that's fine," he replied.

Tatsuya never had any intention of keeping Gatekeeper a secret. It posed no real threat to magicians with high psion levels like him and Miyuki so there wasn't much downside to sharing the spell. That said, he did want to keep it within the Yotsuba clan. Tatsuya wasn't proficient in mental interference magic; he cast Gatekeeper with an entirely different skill. In that respect, he was not the ideal candidate to fine-tune the sequence. It was much more reasonable to entrust that process to the Tsukuba family, which had many mental interference–type magic users. For that reason, Tatsuya had no objections to Maya's proposal. Fumiya looked a bit disappointed, but no one showed any sign of dissent.

In Maya's mind, that settled the Okinawa issue. She took a sip of tea before changing the subject. "Well, then. Let's hear about what happened at today's meeting next."

"Of course," Tatsuya replied.

He proceeded to give a summary. Then he reached the part where some of the attendees suggested using Miyuki to appeal to public opinion. Fumiya and Ayako suddenly burned with resentment.

"They've become *very* familiar with us, haven't they? Maybe it's about time to show the world what we're capable of," Yuuka said sarcastically. The world she referred to was the magical one—the magician community.

"There's no need to feel threatened by them. And there's no need to pander to them, either," Katsushige responded immediately. He, too, felt offended, but in a different way.

Finally, Maya spoke up. "Tatsuya, the Yotsuba clan supports your decision. You may continue to ignore all attempts to take advantage of Miyuki."

There was no trace of either irritation or anger in her voice, but her message was crystal clear.

"You don't mind being at odds with the other twenty-seven families?" Tatsuya ventured.

"Not at all." There was no hesitation. Perhaps Maya was already aware of Tomokazu Saegusa's—and by extension, his entire family's—intentions.

"Should we really just sit back and watch?" Fumiya asked, wanting to know if they should be doing *more*.

"Well, there is no need to be docile once we're attacked, now is there?" Maya replied.

Her response forbade any of the Yotsuba from making the first move. But Tatsuya's uncooperative behavior at the meeting and Maya's policy of ignoring the other clans could already be interpreted as provocation. In that sense, it could be argued that Maya was condoning the use of force.

"But let's not let our guard down," she continued. "We are not invincible, as I am sure you all know. Yotsuba magicians are not absolutely superior."

Everyone in the room internally rolled their eyes at this superfluous reminder. And yet there was a tiny part of all of them conceited enough to think they couldn't lose.

"You should especially be vigilant of the Juumonji clan," Maya said. "And Minoru Kudou."

It was unclear whether she was being sincere. Other than Tatsuya and Katsushige, everyone in the room gave her quizzical looks.

"You can't mean the junior Minoru Kudou at Second High. Does he really pose that much of a threat?" Yuuka asked skeptically.

"He worked with me last autumn to get rid of Gongjin Zhou," Tatsuya said. "I can attest he's definitely someone we want to watch out for."

Katsushige looked surprised. He had read the report on the Gongjin Zhou case and knew about Minoru's cooperation and high combat skill. The boy could maybe pose a threat to magicians at Yuuka's and

Fumiya's level. What astounded Katsushige was that even someone as strong as Tatsuya was wary of the boy.

Katsushige would never question this outright. Doubting Minoru's abilities meant doubting Maya herself. The first time may be forgiven, but the second time would only lead to earning the ire of the clan head. Katsushige knew this well.

Still, a sliver of doubt festered inside him.

"We already saw what the Juumonji family was capable of during the Yokohama Incident," Miyuki cut in. "Do you believe the Tooyama family has a similar level of power?"

This sudden change of topic may have been her way of stopping Katsushige from saying something he might regret.

Maya responded, "Lab Ten claimed it researched area-of-effect spells that generate virtual constructs, but its true purpose was to create magicians to serve as the government's last line of defense. As a result, its products—the Juumonji and Tooyama clans—possess a strength in combat that sets them apart from the other twenty-five families."

This last number wasn't a rudimentary miscalculation on Maya's part. It simply recognized that among the twenty-eight families, the Juumonji, Tooyama, and Yotsuba were in a class of their own.

"The government's last line of defense? Not the capital's?" Miyuki asked.

When referring to the fruits of Lab Ten's research, most people said, "In an emergency, the Juumonji magicians are the capital's last line of defense." This meant that even if the capital came under direct attack, Juumonji magicians would swoop in and save the day.

Rather than dealing with small arms, the Juumonji clan's multiple-barrier magic worked best against tanks, artillery, aircraft, and missiles. The solid magical barriers were so powerful, they could neutralize not only heavy ordnance and bombs, but also hypersonic projectiles and—although these were technically forbidden—tactical nuclear weapons.

They didn't even need to surround the entire metropolitan area with a spell. The barriers would be formed at specific points according to calculated attack trajectories and lines of fire. A bomb, for example, could be encased in a barrier to neutralize the explosion. Juumonji magicians possessed that much precision, speed, and power.

Their ability to protect the city earned them their reputation as the capital's last line of defense. But the true purpose of Lab Ten, Maya had said, was to be the government's last line of defense. Taken at face value, that probably meant the magic of the Tooyama clan was different from that of the Juumonji clan.

"That's right," Maya said. "Didn't you know? The Tooyama clan's magic is designed to protect people."

"I wasn't aware of this, either," Yuuka intervened. "Does that mean the Tooyama clan's magic acts on people individually?"

Maya calmly shook her head. "Not exactly. It creates a barrier for groups of people."

Fumiya stepped back into the conversation. "Do the Tooyama clan's spells use simultaneous targeting or multicast?"

"That is something I do not know," Maya answered. She was smiling, but Tatsuya could sense it was dangerous to push this topic any further.

"Then it's decided," he said, putting an end to things. "I'll be especially careful when dealing with the Juumonji clan, the Tooyama clan, and Minoru Kudou."

Similarly, sensing a tension in the air, Katsushige decided not to drag out the conversation about the Tooyama clan's magic. Instead, he returned to the previous topic, expressing concern about Maya's policy toward other clans.

"That aside, are you sure we want to take a confrontational stance against the other families?" he pressed. "Of course we can't let them turn Miyuki into a walking advertisement, but I don't think it's wise to completely abandon any attempts at cooperation with the other clans when it comes to dealing with the anti-magic movements."

"There won't be any confrontation if they don't make anymore foolish moves," Yuuka said, cutting in. "But don't you see we can't cooperate with them unless they apologize to us? I mean, they tried to use our heiress, for goodness' sake. Someone has to teach them a lesson."

Katsuhige stared at her in dismay. "You surprise me, Yuuka. Why do you have to be so aggressive? I can agree it's important to air our grievances, but isolating ourselves won't do us any favors."

"I don't know about that." This time, it was Fumiya who spoke. "Isolating ourselves from society in general may be fatal, but would stepping away from *magic* society really do us much harm? Besides, we're talking about a handful of the twenty-eight families here. That's only a fraction of magic society as we know it. I don't see the need to worry about complete isolation."

Fumiya's argument struck a chord. Maybe it was because of his youthful inexperience. Or his tendency to remove all of the potentially confusing distractions from his field of vision when it suited him.

Access to the products of a civilized society was indispensable for the Yotsuba clan's continued existence. But when it came to everything related to magic, they were perfectly fine on their own. Even if they found themselves in a sticky situation with the USNA Stars, which considered itself the world's most powerful magic unit, the Yotsuba clan could easily fend for itself.

Fumiya continued. "When push comes to shove, we must support Tatsuya and Miyuki with the combined power of the main and branch families, even if it means all-out war with the other Numbers."

"My instructions will not change," Maya maintained. "Ignore all attempts to turn the Yotsuba heiress into an icon to be paraded through the streets. And if you are attacked, feel free to fight back at your own discretion."

Leaving her agreement with Fumiya ambiguous, she ended the discussion there.

◇ ◇ ◇

Saburou's shoulders heaved with heavy breaths. He could no longer stand. And yet he still faced Erika with a defiant spark in his eye, firmly meeting her gaze. Erika's lips twisted into a smile for a brief moment, and then—she was gone. All of a sudden, the small sheath sword at Saburou's waist flew out.

He heard two dry thuds to his left. Shifting to the right, he turned his body toward the sound and shielded his face with the wooden *wakizashi* in his dominant hand. Just in time. Erika's sword made contact with his wrist.

"You're getting better," she said, lowering her weapon.

Saburou stood down. There was no pain in his wrist.

After sparring with Leo, Erika took over. In their training, she and Saburou were stopping their weapons just before striking their opponents to avoid causing injury. Rather than a standard spar, the main focus was to create opportunities for Saburou to get practice.

Erika would attack just to the point where Saburou couldn't keep up. Then Saburou would use his psychokinesis to give him time to defend and line up a counterattack. After that, the cycle would repeat.

"Now we're really done for the day," Erika said. "Don't forget to do a cooldown."

"Shthank you!" Saburou hollered, lowering his head and fumbling the words out of exaustion. Before he could look up, Erika was gone. Presumably to take a shower.

Saburou's body slumped to the floor as if his back had given out. He hadn't sustained any fresh injuries, but the training had been so intense, his entire body was feeling it. Leo watched the hunched-over younger boy gasp for air, but his thoughts were on Erika.

She turns into a completely different person when instructing Saburou, he mused. *I can't put my finger on how exactly she's different, but she definitely wasn't like this when she was teaching me Usuba Kagerou.*

Erika was clearly serious about making Saburou stronger. But she was focused on teaching him strength, not technique. At least that was how Leo saw it. For her, this was completely out of character.

* * *

Leo was only at the Chiba dojo today because Erika had asked him to be Saburou's training partner. Actually, he saw it as more of a demand than a request, but that was beside the point. Ultimately, there was no reason for overstaying his welcome now that Saburou's training was over. He briefly said his goodbyes to the long-haired boy, who was still too exhausted to get up, and headed to the apprentice shower room.

One time, Leo had been tricked into going into Erika's shower room. The price for getting a glimpse of Erika in a towel was a hazing from the other dojo members so brutal that it made the pits of hell seem lukewarm. Sure, he felt kind of lucky in a way. But in the end, embarrassment won out, and he vowed never to go through something like that again.

In the past, a quick dip in the tub might have been enough for dojo visitors to rinse off their sweat, but in this day and age, a hot shower was a must. The Chiba dojo was large enough to have a shower room divided into fourteen private booths, each including their own shower and changing room. There was no segregation by gender due to the overwhelming majority of male members, but each booth could be locked, eliminating the need to worry about voyeurs and perverts. Women could use the bathroom in the main building if they wanted, so the dojo's shower rooms were usually used by only men.

When Leo entered the shower room, only one booth was in use. Not paying much attention, he walked into the front booth with his change of clothes.

If someone had no particular preferences, they could clean up in three minutes with the shower's automatic setting. Leo stood under the showerhead. After running his fingers through his hair, scrubbing his face with his palms, and letting the machine do the rest, he was done. He had to dry off and get dressed by himself, of course. But the entire process only took five minutes.

He stepped directly out of the shower booth to a long horizontal mirror and simple dresser that extended across the width of the wall.

He usually let his hair dry naturally, but this day he decided to pick up a blow-dryer on a whim.

He was currently dressed in a tank top and shorts. His jacket was still stored in a locker. Since it was mid-April, Leo's outfit was too chilly on its own outdoors, but the shower room was warm enough.

Suddenly, the urge came over him. He made two strong fists in the mirror. Then he stuck his chest out, raised his left and right arms at shoulder height, and bent them at the elbows. Behold—the front double biceps pose.

Next, he put his hands on his hips, shoulders foward, and broadened his upper back into a front lat spread. His well-developed back muscles created a nice inverted triangle. The perfect V shape.

With elbows bent and arms in front of his body, Leo then leaned forward to expand the trapezius muscles at the base of his neck—the most muscular pose.

Finally, he returned to a single-armed flex and gazed down at his muscular tricep with a satisfied sigh.

"What are you doing?"

"Gah!"

Leo had been so focused on making poses in the mirror that he hadn't noticed Erika appear beside him.

"And with a dryer in hand, no less," she said teasingly.

Leo's embarrassment for getting caught making poses quickly changed when he caught a glimpse of Erika's outfit.

"Wh-what are you wearing?!" he shouted, unable to look her in the face.

She had on a tank top just long enough to cover the rise in her chest, and her shorts were short enough to be mistaken for underwear, revealing her supple thighs. Leo could see the small of her back, her muscular limbs, and the flushed skin of her cleavage all in plain view.

"What do you mean?" Erika asked incredulously. "This is a perfectly acceptable outfit to wear after a shower. I'm even wearing underwear underneath."

"D-don't tell me that!" Leo screeched, his face in his palms. "What are you doing here anyway?"

"I'm allowed, aren't I?" She pouted. "It was too much of a hassle to go to the main building."

She flopped down a seat away from Leo and picked up a blow-dryer.

"Go on and dry your hair," she continued. "And don't worry. I'll keep your little bodybuilder show a secret."

"N-no, I'm good!"

Leo dropped the blow-dryer on the dresser and stumbled out of the shower room. Erika shrugged and proceeded to dry her hair. Once she was done, she slipped a tunic over her clothes and headed to her room.

The tea party–style debriefing continued with Tatsuya shifting the conversation to the offensive magic he believed to be Tuman Bomba.

"So, not even you could distinguish the identity of the attacker?" Katsushige asked.

Tatsuya nodded. "That's correct."

"But if the spell you encountered was truly Tuman Bomba…" Katsushige paused. "That would mean the New Soviet Union is putting the long-distance remote sighting system to practical use."

"Is that the same kind of system as Third Eye?" Yuuka asked.

"Yes," Katsushige affirmed before turning to Maya. "Based on the presumed nature of the spell Tatsuya encountered, it doesn't seem to need Third Eye's precision. However, it does seem capable of calculating the variables involved in duplicating magic sequences countless times and then triggering them simultaneously. This is not something that can be accomplished by a single magician. The New Soviets are most likely using a complex system that involves a powerful computer capable of calculation support."

"Hmm…" Maya pondered. "What do you think, Tatsuya?"

"That's a reasonable assumption. I would even suggest a large CAD is capable of integrating all the functions Katsushige mentioned. It can also create activation sequences to lighten the magician's burden."

"Are you saying all the magician needs to do to cast the spell is load an activation sequence into their device?" Maya asked.

"Yes, the process could definitely be automatic once the sequence has been loaded," Tatsuya confirmed.

"But does that really ease the burden on the magician?" Yuuka challenged. "If even the process of loading of the activation sequence is automated, I feel it's possible the magician could be forced to perform magic beyond their limits."

"The CAD won't cast magic beyond what the magician is capable of," Tatsuya assured her. "As long as no Boosters are attached, that is."

"By 'Boosters,' do you mean those Sorcery Boosters supplied by the Hong Kong Mafia?" Yuuka asked. "I thought the organization that created them was destroyed."

"It was, but I'm sure the manufacturing method is still out there somewhere," Tatsuya responded. "This is all purely theoretical, of course."

"Of course," Maya interjected, putting an end to Yuuka's questions. "I am also interested in how the magic works, but there is something more pressing than that."

She turned to Miyuki, daring the heiress to read her mind. This was Maya's idea of training her successor.

"I believe the most urgent issue on the table is how to stop the spell," Miyuki replied confidently. Luckily, she had a similar conversation with Tatsuya the night before.

Maya gave her successor a satisfied nod. She didn't know Miyuki had reached that conclusion with Tatsuya's guidance, but she probably wouldn't have cared.

"Let's put aside for a moment whether this spell is, in fact, Tuman Bomba or not," she proposed. "What matters is that it produces oxyhydrogen and then ignites it. How would you stop it, Miyuki?"

This topic had been brought up on the VTOL ride to the main house, so Miyuki was again prepared.

"If we can pinpoint the precise moment the spell activates, we should be able to stop it with Freeze Flame," she offered. "But that is probably easier said than done."

Freeze Flame was a spell that prevented combustion by limiting the amount of heat in an object. Even if Tuman Bomba combined hydrogen and oxygen to cause an explosion *without* heat, as long as heat was produced as a by-product of that process, Freeze Flame could prevent that increase in heat.

"Interesting," Maya murmured. "How would you stop Tuman Bomba, Katsushige?"

"Well," he began, "that depends on the breadth of the spell. But ultimately, separating the oxygen from the hydrogen immediately after they have formed via density manipulation should render it ineffective."

Maya turned her attention to Fumiya. "Any ideas?"

"The only thing I'm capable of is putting up a barrier to withstand it," he admitted. "But I think my sister's Polar Dispersal could prevent the spell from activating."

An air of optimism formed as each person in the room described how they would neutralize Tuman Bomba. Just then, Tatsuya spoke up.

"Sure, it's theoretically possible to stop the spell via methods such as density manipulation and Polar Dispersal," he said. "The problem is, as Miyuki mentioned, whether we can get the timing right. Tuman Bomba's high-speed chain of magic sequence restoration, which I refer to as chain casting for convenience, makes it extremely difficult for us to complete our spells before Tuman Bomba is cast."

"But this spell we're assuming to be Tuman Bomba requires an expanse of water equal to its attack range, right?" Yuuka interjected. "That's easy to do out at sea or on a lake, but what if the target is on land? Wouldn't it be necessary to create fog or puddles of water beforehand? That could make it more predictable."

There was something in Yuuka's tone of voice that made Tatsuya think she wasn't really arguing a point at all. But he chose not to comment on that and said instead: "If I were the magician casting this spell, I would aim for a rainy day. Probably not ideal in the deserts of the Middle East, but in Japan it would not be difficult to find an opportunity."

Yuuka shrugged at him. Tatsuya wasn't sure what she meant by this or even what she was thinking. He hesitated for a moment before deciding it wasn't worth his time.

"Again, chain casting is extremely fast," he continued. "Unless you can time your counterattack perfectly, it would be better to simply defend with barrier magic."

At the mention of barrier magic, everyone—with the exception of the Shiba siblings— turned their attention to the girl standing silently behind Miyuki's chair. Minami recoiled under the intense scrutiny.

When he got home, Leo entered his room and made a beeline for his visiphone. There was something that had been bothering him all the way home. It was something he had trouble coming to terms with, and now he couldn't resist the urge to talk to someone about it.

After several seconds of ringing, the visiphone screen brightened, revealing a very Japanese-looking study. Considering that the owner of the room was a high school student, calling it a study room might be more appropriate. But the room—with its shelves that extended to the ceiling and were stuffed full of paper books, which were rare in this day and age—certainly fit the description of a study.

"Hey, Leo. You never call me." It was Mikihiko.

"Hey, Mikihiko," Leo said weakly. "Do you have a minute?"

Mikihiko quickly noticed his friend's uncharacteristically downcast expression and became worried. *"...What's wrong?"*

"There's something I want your opinion on."

Just as things were getting serious, Mikihiko's microphone picked up an unexpected voice: "Yoshida, your bath is— Oops, sorry."

The voice belonged to a girl and sounded faraway. Most likely near the study entrance. If that wasn't enough, Leo caught a glimpse of Mizuki's face as it popped up briefly in the background of his screen.

"Sorry!" He panicked. "Is this a bad time? I'll call you later."

He was just about to hang up when Mikihiko stopped him with the same level of panic in his voice.

"Hold on, Leo! This isn't what it looks like!"

"You don't have to keep secrets from me," Leo mumbled. "I'm mature enough to know that just because Mizuki is in your house, you're not up to anything indecent."

"Wh-what do you mean by 'indecent'?" Mikihiko pressed.

"Oh, you know. Something involving the birds and the bees…"

"O-of course we're not doing anything like that!" Mikihiko stammered. *"Shibata isn't that kind of girl!"*

"That's why I said you're *not* up to anything like that!" Leo insisted.

Just as the confusion was reaching its peak, Mizuki appeared in Mikihiko's background once again.

"*Yoshida?*" she asked. *"Did you call my name?"*

This time, she wasn't alone. A different girl showed up in the background with her.

"*Mizuki! Are you ready yet?*" this second girl called.

Leo recognized her. If his memory served him right, she was in his class and a member of the art club.

"*Oh, are you on the phone, Yoshida? We can save the ice sculpting for later and work on something else in the meantime, since it's on a tight schedule.*" The girl grabbed Mizuki's arm and pulled her out of the room.

As soon as the girls disappeared, Leo asked tentatively, "Don't tell me…are all of the art club members at your place?"

"That's right," Mikihiko replied. *"It's not just Shibata. So nothing involving birds and bees can happen today."*

Does that mean it could happen if it was just the two of them? Leo wondered. But he thought it best not to say anything else that could potentially offend his friend.

Instead he said, "Sorry for doubting you."

"It's fine," Mikihiko sighed. *"So what did you want my opinion on?"*

Leo honestly felt awkward about asking for advice after that uncomfortable misunderstanding. But if he could keep the matter to himself, he would never have made this call in the first place.

"It's not a big deal…" he began.

Mikihiko nodded. *"I'm listening."*

"But, well, I feel like Erika has been acting strangely lately and wanted to hear what you think."

"Did something happen between you two?"

"Not exactly." Leo paused. "But she called me to her family's dojo today."

"Why the dojo?" his friend puzzled.

"She wanted me to help her train this freshman that has caught her eye," Leo explained. "After all that effort she put into helping me learn Usuba Kagerou, I couldn't say no. Besides, I was curious about the freshman."

"That freshman wouldn't happen to be Saburou Yaguruma, would it?"

Leo looked surprised. "You know him?"

"I spoke to him briefly after the entrance ceremony," Mikihiko explained. *"So those rumors about Erika taking Yaguruma under her wing were true. How is it going?"*

"She's teaching him a lot," Leo said. "And being really thorough about it."

"Wow, that's…different."

Mikihiko was more than a little surprised to hear this. He knew Erika's policy was strictly *steal techniques, don't expect to be taught.*

"Right?" Leo appealed. "People told me her teaching style was a little unusual with me, too, but with Saburou, it's *fundamentally* different. She isn't trying to teach him techniques. She's trying to make him stronger."

"That's not like her at all."

A worried frown appeared on Mikihiko's face. He had known Erika for even longer than Leo, so his concern was twice as great.

Leo hesitated before starting again. "Then, there's this thing where I bumped into her in the shower after practice."

"What happened there?" Mikihiko asked with sobering intensity.

Leo paused, meeting his friend's serious gaze. Then he clarified, "I'm talking about the shower room in the dojo. The one apprentices use."

"…Oh. Gotcha," Mikihiko replied. *"So what happened?"*

"Well, Erika came out of the shower in a crop top and shorts so short… She was practically in a swimsuit!"

"Geez. I'm surprised you survived." Mikihiko shivered with genuine fear for his friend's life.

"Thank you!" Leo stared at his screen, dead serious. "I knew you'd understand."

"Wait, what?" Mikihiko was suddenly confused.

"I didn't see Erika's underwear today, but she was definitely showing a lot of skin," Leo said. "And yet she was completely calm when I saw her like that! She didn't even bat an eye! Isn't that strange?"

"Uh, Leo? I think you're reading into this way too much. Erika's always like that."

"Yeah, I know. But isn't that *strange*?"

"……"

Mikihiko didn't know what to say. It was now crystal clear. His friend's situation was far more serious than he thought.

Leo continued, "Anyway, I'm afraid she's pushing herself too hard. Ever since her brother died, she's been acting like everything's okay, but I don't buy it. Every day must be rough."

"I'm sure it is," Mikihiko began slowly. *"But what does that have to do with Erika acting strange?"*

"This is just a hunch," Leo explained. "But I think Erika is trying to get revenge."

"For her brother, you mean?"

Leo nodded.

"But who could be her target?" Mikihiko puzzled. "*Toshikazu died at the hands of the gang responsible for the Hakone terrorist attack. All of those guys are dead.*"

The only thing announced to the public was that the whereabouts of the Hakone terrorist mastermind remained unknown. However, the Chiba family, whose eldest son was killed during the incident, were mostly told the truth. Leo and Mikihiko were also given an overview of the incident on the condition that they didn't speak of it to anyone else.

"I think her target might be Tatsuya," Leo confided.

"*What?!*" Mikihiko was shocked by this unexpected answer, but he quickly pushed back against his friend's theory. "*Leo, Tatsuya had nothing to do with Toshikazu's death. Sure, he stopped Erika's brother in a sense, but he also freed Toshikazu from the clutches of the bad guys. The Chiba family is grateful for everything Tatsuya did.*"

"That, my friend, doesn't matter," Leo lectured. "Logic goes right out the window when emotions take over."

Mikihiko fell silent.

"But don't worry. I don't actually think Erika is trying to *kill* Tatsuya," Leo admitted.

"*For crying out loud, Leo! I thought you were serious!*" Mikihiko groaned.

"Hey, my bad," Leo said. "Anyway, what I wanted to ask you is if you think Erika is getting too headstrong. You've known her for a lot longer than I have, so I thought you might have noticed something."

"*What do you mean by 'headstrong'?*"

"How should I put this? Well, the way I see it, she wants to get one over on Tatsuya and she'll do whatever it takes. Like, even if that means throwing away her femininity or whatever, no cost is too great."

Mikihiko let out an exasperated sigh. "*…You're definitely thinking too much now.*" Then he shook his head and continued. "*I doubt Erika is going through anything that extreme. At the same time, I can't say your theories are complete nonsense.*"

Leo gazed at his friend expectantly.

"*Well, we can keep an eye on her for a while,*" Mikihiko suggested.

"Sounds good," Leo agreed.

A sudden scoff escaped his lips, and he shrugged. "She'll probably want to keep using me for training anyway. I couldn't take my eyes off her if I wanted to."

Mikihiko smirked. "*You two make a good pair.*"

"Ugh, shut up," Leo said with a groan and a grimace.

Around that same time, the Saegusa family had invited Minoru over for a late lunch and dinner.

"I already told our brother you're here," Mayumi confided.

"Thank you," Minoru replied.

"We'll take you home by helicopter when we're done," Kasumi chimed in.

"Thank you," Minoru repeated awkwardly. "That's very kind of you."

"It's no problem, Minoru." Izumi smiled. "You know you don't have to be so formal around us."

"I-I'm not being formal," he stammered. "Uh, what about your father?"

He noticed only four places were set at the table—one for Mayumi, Kasumi, Izumi, and himself. Kouichi's cutlery was strangely absent.

The Saegusa girls' father had been absent at lunch, too. Not that Minoru was itching to talk to him. He just thought he should pay his respects.

Mayumi replied in her younger sister's place after checking with the servants. "It seems he went out somewhere after an early dinner with our brother. I'm sorry he didn't greet you before he left."

"No, it's my fault," Minoru said modestly. "I should have said hello when I first got here."

"Hey, didn't Izumi just tell you not to be so formal?" Mayumi scolded lightly. "You're our guest, so please relax."

"Ha-ha, thanks," he said with a relieved smile.

It was rare for him to smile and relax like this. He was usually under a lot of pressure. His outstanding magical abilities were tempered by a sickly body that could leave him bedridden for weeks. He knew all too well the pain of failing to live up to expectations. Even his amazing mind and aggressively good looks that practically forced others to stare became a kind of burden.

Minoru had talent. He had skill.

And yet he couldn't fulfill his responsibilities because of a lack of a healthy body. He couldn't live up to the role he was born to play. These thoughts were slowly driving him mad. The guilt Minoru felt was what drove him to always defer to those around him.

The reason why he could relax around the Saegusa sisters was—first and foremost—because they were indifferent to his good looks. It had been a while since they last met, so he was simultaneously surprised and grateful for the way they immediately treated him as an everyday acquaintance.

They always behaved like this, but it felt so natural now. Little did he know, the reason for this was due to desensitization after being regularly exposed to Miyuki's beauty, which was on par with Minoru's. Some might argue hers was even more refined.

Of course, there was no way he would have realized this. His own first impression of Miyuki was completely focused on her exceptional skill as a magician. Her beauty was secondary. At the same time, those close to Miyuki could still take a keen interest in Minoru's good looks.

Thinking about Miyuki reminded him of the girl who spent a lot of time around Miyuki but still gawked at his face—Minami.

A chuckle escaped his lips. He remembered the time he woke up and saw her scurrying away, her face beet red. Strangely enough, thinking about Minami didn't make him feel uncomfortable.

Usually, blatant stares from girls were suffocating and even depressing at times. Minami should be no different. And yet thinking about her only made Minoru feel relaxed.

He even found her adorable, which was a first for him.

Izumi broke the silence. "What's on your mind, Minoru? You look like you're enjoying yourself."

"Oh, sorry. I was just remembering something." Minoru's cheeks flushed a soft pink. The Saegusa sisters catching him thinking about Minami made him all the more embarrassed.

Kasumi grinned. "It's times like these when I realize you're just like any other normal guy."

No one had ever called him normal. It felt refreshing and nice.

Dinner started off with an innocuous topic, but unfortunately, it didn't stop there. Mayumi had been wondering about a particular incident for some time now and was dying to confirm the details. She questioned Minoru about the condition of a Second High student who had been seriously injured in an anti-magician attack on her way home from school in February.

"Did that student ever recover?" she asked

"She did. Thankfully. There wasn't even a scar," Minoru replied.

"Thank goodness." Izumi sighed.

Though she didn't end up getting hurt, Izumi had also been attacked by an anti-magician fanatic before. The Second High student's case hit very close to home.

"What about the anti-magician?" Kasumi asked. "I bet no one even questioned the attacker."

A hesitant smile played on Minoru's lips. "Well, after looking at the victim's injuries, the authorities determined the student's magic was only used in self-defense."

"Obviously. So they put the attacker in jail, right?" Kasumi asked expectantly.

In her mind, if it was clear the Second High student acted in self-defense, the anti-magician would be dealt a severe sentence.

But Minoru's expression clouded regretfully. "Unfortunately, he was diagnosed as being in a state of drug-induced insanity, and the case was eventually dropped."

"No way!" Kasumi exclaimed. "That Second High student's injuries could have been life-threatening! I thought the insanity defense didn't apply to violent crimes."

"I only heard this secondhand," Minoru prefaced, "but apparently since the victim was a magician and the attacker wasn't, this kind of incident normally wouldn't result in serious injuries. The victim ultimately wasn't even left with a single scar, so the entire thing isn't considered a serious crime."

"Does that mean the assailant isn't guilty just because the victim is a magician?!" Kasumi yelled indignantly.

"Clearly, the law doesn't apply equally to magicians and the so-called general public," Izumi said bitterly.

Neither Kasumi nor Mayumi bothered to debate their younger sister's extreme statement.

"Yeah…" Minoru agreed. In all honesty, he was more indignant about the issue than Izumi was.

Then, in almost a whisper, he murmured, "It's incidents like these that make me wonder if it's impossible for humans and magicians to coexist."

His words didn't reach the Saegusa sisters' ears. If they had known of the despair Minoru expressed on this night, the future may have been different.

Tatsuya, Miyuki, and Minami returned to Tokyo at 8:00 PM. First, they stopped at the rooftop in Chofu, which they had used on the way to the main house. Joined by Katsushige, Kotona, and Kanata, the six passengers descended from the compact VTOL onto the heliport.

Their driver bowed to Tatsuya. "This is where I leave you, Master Tatsuya."

"Thanks, Hanabishi."

"Please. Call me Hyougo. I look forward to seeing you very soon."

Tatsuya wondered when "very soon" would be but didn't ask. He silently watched the VTOL fly away.

"Tatsuya, Miyuki," Katsushige called.

Tatsuya spun around. Miyuki, meanwhile, had been keeping a wary eye on Katsushige's group ever since they boarded the aircraft together.

"Are you two familiar with this building?" Katsushige asked in a businesslike fashion. Neither he nor the other two members of his group seemed bothered by Miyuki's suspicious stares.

"From what I can tell, it seems to be Yotsuba property," Tatsuya answered.

Katsushige tilted his head in a way that indicated Tatsuya was close.

"It's actually the Yotsuba Tokyo base."

"I heard there were plans to build a place like that," Tatsuya said. "So this is it, huh?"

"Yes," Katsushige answered. "The entire residential portion is filled with people with ties to the Yotsuba family. It also functions as temporary lodging for combat personnel in the field."

"Interesting," Tatsuya murmured. "That would explain why it looks like a stronghold."

The building was located in the center of the city, much like a castle. But instead of a moat, it was ringed with layers of security.

Lacking any semblance of a window, the first three office floors were lit by fiber optics. The residential floors four and above were all equipped with wide verandas that made it difficult to see into the building from the outside. A protective fence covered the entire surface of these upper floors, most likely intended not to prevent people from jumping out but to stop intruders from climbing in. Each unit was also likely equipped with armored plates in place of storm shutters.

"The three of us will be moving here soon," Katsushige said.

"I see," Tatsuya responded, unsurprised.

It was completely reasonable for the branch family heirs and heiresses to settle into an expansive building like this.

"And the three of you will be joining us," Kotona added.

This news caught Tatsuya unawares.

"I was told you will have your own personal research facility with even better equipment than you have at your current home," she continued.

"Is that what my aunt said?" Tatsuya asked.

"Yes." Kotona nodded.

"Please tell her we have relayed the message." Katsushige smiled.

With that, the two of them and Kanata entered the building.

Once Tatsuya and Miyuki arrived home, they sat down on the living room sofa and began discussing Katsushige and Kotona's sudden news.

"Did you know this was coming?" Miyuki asked.

After all the stress of the day, there was a natural distance in her gestures and tone, as if she were retreating into the familiar and treating Tatsuya like her brother. The day she would fully speak to him like her fiancé still seemed far away.

"I remember hearing about having to move to the Yotsuba's Tokyo headquarters," Tatsuya admitted. "But I thought it wouldn't be for several months. Aunt Maya must be worried for our safety."

"Does that mean someone is trying to attack us?" Miyuki worried.

Minami entered the room with a tea tray in her hands and a nervous expression on her face.

"Maybe," Tatsuya said. "But I'm willing to bet this move has more to do with preparing for the risk of future exposure."

"Do you really think Aunt Maya will turn against the other twenty-seven families?" Miyuki asked.

"Yes," Tatsuya said gravely. "And she won't stop there."

"Do you mean she may even challenge the government?" Panic surged through Miyuki's voice.

"Well, the government isn't in complete agreement on issues right now, so whatever resistance she might be planning won't be a total confrontation with state power. Besides, if anything like that were to happen, it would be me, not Aunt Maya, pulling the trigger."

"Oh, Tatsuya…" Miyuki anxiously clung to him, and he gently stroked her hand.

"I doubt she has a reason for taking on the entire Japanese government," he said. "The National Defense Force, though, is a whole different beast."

Miyuki's grip tightened. He gave her a reassuring smile and gently stroked her hair.

"Relax. I won't let it turn into a full-scale armed conflict."

"That's comforting to hear," Miyuki said, leaning on him like she used to.

Rather than feeling awkward, Minami, too, felt her anxiety fade away.

[2]

The day after the meeting that brought together the younger members of the twenty-eight families, the Mitsuya family received a troublesome guest.

Her name was Tsukasa Tooyama. Tsukasa was a female noncommissioned officer in the National Defense Force, registered under a last name spelled with characters that didn't give away her magician's rank. In all other circumstances, she used her real name.

This use of an alias was both a violation of the rules of service and a criminal act, but no one condemned her for it. It was military policy to conceal the identity of anyone in the Tooyama family. Even the Tooyama family's magic was a well-kept secret by those in power. This was a necessary precaution to keep its existence hidden from the public and available for government use at any given moment.

The Mitsuya family was connected to the dark underbelly of the world as one of the Ten Master Clans that managed Lab Three. Exceptionally known for their lineage of powerful magicians, the Mitsuya family had engaged in negotiations with foreign powers and often secretly made trips abroad with the government's tacit consent. The information the family acquired was beneficial to the National Defense Force. They also secretly supplied weapons to foreign armed forces, facilitating the Japanese government's promotion of desirable military actions.

The relationship between the Mitsuya family and the National Defense Force was not quite one of give-and-take. The latter party profited from the connection substantially more. Nonetheless, because of their ties to the National Defense Force, the Mitsuya family found themselves in a position where they had to consider the military's intentions. This, among other things, made it clear that magicians and politicians were not on equal footing.

Tsukasa was a magician of the same twenty-eight families that the Mitsuya belonged to. Since the Tooyama family was never elected to be one of the Ten Master Clans, they were below the Mitsuya in the pecking order. However, the Mitsuya could not afford to neglect Tsukasa Tooyama, given her deep connection to high-ranking staff in the National Defense Force. In fact, the relationships connecting the Mitsuya family, the National Defense Force, and Tsukasa essentially required the Mitsuya to heed Tsukasa's requests, assuming they weren't too demanding. Shiina and Tsukasa were only acquainted in the first place because the Mitsuya had to accommodate the Tooyama family as a general rule.

Naturally, the adults in the Mitsuya family who fully understood the implications of their relationship did not care much for Tsukasa. She herself knew this but couldn't care less whether she was liked or not.

"I apologize for bothering you at such a busy time." Tsukasa bowed politely.

"Don't worry about it. Just state your business," the Mitsuya clan head, Gen Mitsuya, said. He clearly wanted to wrap up this meeting as quickly as possible.

His eldest son, Motoharu, sent him a reproachful look, but Gen didn't seem to notice. The Mitsuya clan head's attention was focused entirely on Tsukasa.

"I came here to talk to you about yesterday's meeting," she said, indicating she was not in a hurry.

"I see," Gen replied, sullenly resigning himself to his fate.

Fearing this conversation may end in a fight if he left it entirely up to his father, Motoharu joined in. Somewhat cheerfully, he said, "We were under the impression you attended the meeting."

"My younger brother takes care of all clan matters," Tsukasa replied mechanically.

Despite her pleasant smile, she failed to truly answer the question. Luckily, Motoharu knew all about how the Tooyama clan operated.

He let her reply pass without comment and moved on to the next question. "So what do you want to know about the meeting?"

"I heard it was very pleasant and many friendships were deepened," she replied.

"Yes, it was great," Motoharu agreed.

"Unfortunately, I also heard the harmonious mood turned unbearably sour thanks to a certain someone," Tsukasa hinted.

"It wasn't that bad," Motoharu said with a neutral tone.

"Really?" Tsukasa shot him an icy stare. "A little bird told me the Yotsuba family representative didn't even attend the subsequent luncheon."

"He had a prior commitment," Motoharu explained.

He only defended Tatsuya because he didn't want to play any part in a potential feud between the Tooyama and Yotsuba clans. If Tsukasa concluded that Tatsuya was disrupting the magicians' unity, the Mitsuya clan would be obligated to support her next course of action. In Motoharu's mind, that would be a complete waste of energy. Unfortunately, Tsukasa had already drawn her conclusions.

"We have been worried about Tatsuya Shiba's uncooperative behavior for a while now," she said.

"When you say 'we,' are you speaking on behalf of the National Defense Force?" Motoharu asked.

"Precisely. It has come to our attention that we must test whether Tatsuya jeopardizes public safety."

Unable to let Tsukasa's comment slide, Gen stepped back into the conversation: "Tatsuya isn't a soldier. The National Defense Force has no authority to test him, the Yotsuba clan, the Tooyama clan, or any of the Ten Master Clan magicians, for that matter."

"Authority or not, we can still run tests." Tsukasa smiled. There wasn't an ounce of warmth in her eyes.

"So what do you want from us?" Gen pressed.

Clearly, he had no choice but to become a part of Tsukasa's devious plan. His defeated question brought a superficially friendly smile to Tsukasa's lips.

"We would like you to let us borrow Shiina for our exercises," she answered.

This caught Gen off guard, his face paling.

Tsukasa continued. "Don't worry. There is nothing dangerous about the exercise. Besides, we already have Shiina's consent."

"When did that happen?" Motoharu stammered in dismay.

Gen clicked his tongue bitterly. He was no longer in the mood to care about how rude he appeared.

"I doubt I have the right to refuse anyway," he spat.

"Of course you do." She smiled. "I'd love to have your enthusiastic cooperation in this little venture."

Her tone—which was nothing less than shameless—made Gen click his tongue again. But this last gesture was nothing more than an expression of submission.

After the school day was over at First High, Tatsuya briefly stopped by the student council to say hello. With Miyuki's permission, he then headed to the robot research club's garage. He wasn't on his daily rounds. Nor was he planning to borrow the robot club's room for maintenance on Pixie—which he sometimes did. He was headed to the club because Takuma Shippou had called him there.

"Hello, Tatsuya. Sorry for making you come all this way," Takuma said.

"No problem," Tatsuya replied. "I heard you have a secret for me."

"It's not exactly a secret." Takuma hesitated. "I just didn't want the student council president to overhear."

"So what is it?" Tatsuya pressed.

"It has to do with what happened after you left the Youth Council."

"Let me guess," Tatsuya sighed. "Everyone went to town bad-mouthing me."

"I wouldn't exactly say they went to town…"

So the bad-mouthing part is true, Tatsuya thought.

"Tatsuya…" Takuma began. "You knew your comment would anger the other council members and sour the mood. Why would you do something to turn everyone against you?"

Tatsuya had no social or moral obligation to answer Takuma's question. He simply offered it on a whim. Or perhaps as a gift to Takuma for being kind enough to keep him informed.

"The powerful might try to gain favor with the weak," he said, "but the fears of the weak will never disappear unless the very power that threatens them is abandoned."

"In other words, as long as we're magicians, it's inevitable for us to be feared and envied by the general public?" Takuma offered.

"Well, non-magicians don't always envy magicians," Tatsuya amended. "But it's unavoidable that they fear us. To them, we're essentially carrying guns when everyone else is unarmed."

"Is that why you were opposed to the social appeals?" Takuma asked. "Because there's no point?"

"I only objected to that because everyone clearly wanted to put the Yotsuba clan heiress in the line of fire," Tatsuya asserted.

"I don't think that was their intention," Takuma said, as if defending someone in particular. Then he paused before admitting: "But I *do* agree it was a blatant way to lead the discussion."

This last statement was critical of Tomokazu's methods, perhaps reflecting the shared history of the Saegusa and Shippou.

Tatsuya spoke up again. "Shippou. You know as well as I do that even if we act on good intentions, it doesn't mean those good intentions will be returned."

"I guess that's true," Takuma conceded. "And I see what you're saying."

"Good. Because even if magicians cater to non-magicians, there's no guarantee they'll be grateful for it. The possibility of their jealousy building up and getting set off isn't limited to a pessimist's nightmare."

"You mean our relationship with non-magicians will eventually lead to open hostility? Aren't you—?" Takuma was about to suggest Takuya was overthinking things but trailed off. Midsentence, he realized that saying such things was just a way to fool himself.

"Sure, I admit it," Tatsuya said. "Slapping my fiancée's face on a billboard to appeal to the public would yield a certain level of success. She is beautiful, after all. And since beauty is a strong enough selling point on its own, we wouldn't even need to invoke the 3B Principle."

The 3B Principle was a rule of thumb that stated that beauty, beasts (aka animals), and babies are the three elements in advertising that effectively win the attention and favor of consumers. These elements were not limited to advertisements, of course. Especially when it came to beautiful women. Many men were attracted to beautiful women, and in turn, women were influenced by the portrayal of beauty in media.

"The problem is," Tatsuya continued, "the more effective a publicity campaign, the more resistant people are to it. In this case, we could even call these resistant people fanatics. If everything goes as the Saegusa family wants, Miyuki will become the target of those fanatics. I can't let that happen. It's completely out of the question."

"I understand how you feel," Takuma said. "But you should have said all this at the Youth Council. I don't think it was a good idea to stir everyone up without an explanation."

"You have a point, Shippou," Tatsuya responded. But that didn't mean he agreed. Tatsuya had enough foresight to consider everything Takuma mentioned before acting the way he did.

"Then again," he continued, "if the Saegusa family had been talked into using Miyuki at the meeting, it probably would have caused stronger animosity in the long run. By acting the bad guy, I helped the Saegusa save face."

Takuma blinked in silence. That had not even crossed his mind.

Tatsuya continued. "I'm not against magicians promoting their contributions to society. I just think we should consider all the risks involved. Extremists who realize society doesn't support them will act in catastrophic ways. They will try to eliminate what they consider to be evil, even if it means destroying themselves in the process."

"What do you mean by 'evil'?" Takuma asked.

Tatsuya explained. "Imagine there is a powerful person who is different from us. We can't parade him around as our protector precisely because he is different. For all we know, he could hurt us, and we wouldn't be able to fight back in any way. It doesn't matter whether he actually intends to harm us or not. The mere prospect of him endangering our lives makes us want to get rid of him. If we have to put that person into a category, it would undoubtedly be evil."

"Are you saying anti-magicians consider magicians evil?" Takuma prompted.

Tatsuya shrugged. "That's how it seems to me. That isn't to say magicians have absolute power, but it's safe to say we're stronger than non-magicians when it comes to fighting. The weak don't trust the strong since the latter can overwhelm the former at any given moment."

"So the weak want to see the strong as evil to escape the fear of not knowing when they might be attacked," Takuma reflected.

That's why Tatsuya couldn't bear Miyuki being made a symbol of that evil, he thought. At last, he felt as if he understood the cause of his senior's apprehension.

"Right. As long as we're more powerful, catering to the violence of the weak won't help the situation," Tatsuya said. "That said, it's impossible for us to put an end to this conflict by simply abandoning our strength. Magic is a power innate to magicians. We can't just give that up whenever we want."

"Then, Tatsuya…" Takuma hesitated. "Do you believe it's hopeless for magicians and non-magicians to coexist?"

"Coexistence is extremely difficult for those who don't want to coexist," Tatsuya replied.

With this parting tautological answer, he took his leave. Takuma, however, didn't feel that Tatsuya was saying anything but what he considered to be the truth.

The sun had begun to set, and it was soon time to leave school. After wrapping up his club activities, Leo headed to the cafeteria for a light snack. On the way there, he exchanged greetings with some students he knew; he was popular enough to know about 66 percent of the school's juniors and seniors. Once at the cafeteria, he used a meal ticket with an IC tag to pick up a sandwich at the automated counter and opted for a free water. Then he looked for an empty table and spotted a freshman he had been seeing a lot of lately.

"Hey, Saburou. Can I sit here?"

"Oh, hi, Saijou!" Saburou said, startled. "Yes, of course."

Saburou had been staring so pensively into his empty coffee cup that he only noticed Leo when the older boy called his name.

"Thanks," Leo replied, and took a seat across the table. "Were you waiting for someone?"

"Yeah. Shiina," Saburou said.

I should have known, Leo thought.

Ever since they became training partners, Saburou had told Leo everything about his situation. That included him getting fired as a bodyguard before entering First High. The topic didn't make Leo feel awkward at all, but he decided to change the subject anyway.

"Did Erika give you another tough time today?" he asked.

"Well...same old," Saburou answered vaguely.

Although not visibly injured, he was pretty worn out. So much so, in fact, that Leo worried whether Saburou could protect his childhood friend if something happened on the way home. Then again, the older boy reminded himself, that was none of his business.

The fact that Saburou had been removed as Shiina's bodyguard meant there had been some sort of change, of course. But it also meant the Mitsuya family should be responsible for Shiina's safety, not Saburou. At least until Saburou became Shiina's bodyguard again.

"But I'm grateful," Saburou continued. "Erika's training helps me grow stronger. I even feel bad that she's going to the trouble of helping me when I'm so inexperienced."

"I wouldn't worry about that," Leo said. "She's only training you because she wants to."

Suddenly, a voice called out. "You're not wrong, Leo, but it kind of pisses me off to hear you say it."

"Whoa!" Leo practically jumped out of his seat.

It was none other than Erika—speak of the devil. In fact, she was standing right behind Leo. Saburou should have noticed her, but for some reason, he seemed even more surpised than his training partner.

"Damn it, Erika!" Leo cursed. "Don't hide your presence and sneak up on us like that. You're not a freaking ninja."

"The art of concealing your presence isn't exclusive to ninjas," Erika lectured. "It's also an essential skill for CQB fighters."

"Yeah, I'm not buying that..." Leo grumbled, sliding down in his seat. His comical posture elicited a giggle from someone behind Erika.

"Oh, hey, Mizuki," Leo greeted. "I didn't see you there."

"That's because I just got here," she said.

Saburou began to squirm in his chair. The arrival of a senior girl he had never met made him uncomfortable. Before he was able to make a run for it, Erika stopped him in his tracks.

"Saburou," she said. "This is Mizuki Shibata. Unlike the three of us, she's a peaceful member of our student body, so don't go dragging her into anything dangerous."

Before he knew what he was doing, Saburou defensively rose to his feet.

"I would never do that!" he yelled. Then he pulled himself together and stiffly bowed at the waist. "I mean, it's nice to meet you. I'm Saburou Yaguruma."

Mizuki laughed to herself at his jumpiness.

"Hello, Saburou. I'm Mizuki," she said with a heartwarming kindness that reminded him of Shiina.

Erika interrupted. "Hey, what are you blushing for?"

"I-I'm not blushing!" Saburou stammered.

"Don't even think about it," Erika said. "Mizuki is Miki's girl."

Mizuki blushed self-conciously. "Erika!"

Suddenly, a new boy's voice cut into the conversation. "My name is Mikihiko, not Miki. Were you talking about me?"

Mikihiko appeared at the cafeteria entrance, apparently just having arrived. His ability to only hear his own name among the many sounds in the room was clearly a result of the cocktail party effect. It seemed to prove that, despite his negations, he had accepted his nickname deep down.

Erika smirked, but Mizuki stopped her before she could speak. "It's nothing!" the girl screeched.

"Whoa, there," Mikihiko said, taken aback by her volume.

She blushed. "Oh, I…"

Erika shook her head at the awkward couple. Not wanting her friend to suffer any longer, she decided to change the subject.

"Hey, Miki," she said. "Is it okay for the disciplinary committee president to slack off in a place like this?"

Mikihiko frowned, but he understood what Erika was doing.

"After-school activities are almost over." He shrugged. "Besides, I'm allowed to take a break once in a while."

"Your schedule must be pretty relaxed, then," Erika teased. "I thought things were going to be hectic with all the freshman recruitment for clubs."

"Things are a lot calmer than in past years," Mikihiko explained. "It's been a big weight off the disciplinary committee's shoulders."

The blush on Mizuki's cheeks finally receded.

"Really?" she asked, surprised. She had no idea what the recruitment competition was like this year, since she wasn't competing for the attention of new students. Instead, she was in charge of responding to applicants brought to each club via the recruiting team.

"It must be thanks to Miyuki," Erika said with an impish smirk. "Even without the Yotsuba name to support her, all the incoming freshmen noticed at the entrance ceremony that she wasn't just another ordinary student."

Erika's amusement must have been contagious, because Mikihiko's face also twisted into a wry grin.

"It's thanks to Tatsuya, too," he said. "He has the eyes of a hawk. No matter how much the juniors and seniors let loose, they always stand at attention whenever he's around."

"I don't think he's a scary person, though," Mizuki defended cautiously.

"No," Mikihiko agreed. "He isn't oppressive. It's just impossible to ignore him. I'm not sure if it's a type of charisma or what exactly. But when he enters a room, everyone's eyes are on him."

"What's he like?" Saburou interjected. After failing to escape the room, he had been sitting in silence so as not to disturb the conversation. But now he spoke up. Tatsuya had put him through a painful experience, but Saburou didn't hold it against him. This question didn't stem from a place of resentment, either. He just wanted to get to know the guy in Shiina's student council circle.

He didn't address his question to Mikihiko alone; it was addressed to everyone present. The four seniors exchanged glances, trying to decide who would answer.

Ultimately, Mikihiko spoke up first. "He's a brilliant guy. And his magic expertise is already beyond college level."

"He's strong, too," Erika added. "His performance during mock battles isn't anything to write home about, but when push comes to shove, he becomes a force to be reckoned with. I bet his magic is even greater than he lets on."

Leo was next: "But he isn't just a pro at magic; he's physically strong, too. I'm pretty confident in myself, but I would never want to go head-to-head with Tatsuya. I doubt I would come out of something like that alive."

"But he really isn't a scary person," Mizuki repeated, believing what the others had said was over-the-top. "He can be a downright gentleman, really. And he isn't arrogant at all. But that's not what you're asking. What exactly do you want to know, Yaguruma?"

Saburou was stumped. He wasn't expecting to get a question in return. Or maybe he just wasn't sure exactly what he was trying to ask.

Erika tried to help. "If you're curious about Tatsuya's personality, I'd say he's someone who always has his priorities straight. They're very clear in his mind. And no matter how much others threaten or scoff at him, no matter how much someone may shed tears at his feet or entice him with sex appeal, he never strays from those priorities. In fact, he *refuses* to veer away. It makes him the most trustworthy person I know. And the most heartless."

Leo and Mikihiko maintained an awkward silence. Mizuki cautiously said, "Erika…" in an almost reproachful way, but Erika refused to back down.

"Miyuki is Tatsuya's first and foremost priority," she continued. "That's an irrefutable fact. If he had to choose between saving Miyuki or all of us here, he would pick Miyuki without a moment's hesitation."

"Hey…" Leo protested.

"That's..." Mikihiko began. But the two boys were at a loss for words.

Blunt wording aside, they both knew Erika was right.

Saburou had heard a summary of what happened at the Youth Council meeting, and everything suddenly became crystal clear.

So that's why Tatsuya got so mad, he thought.

On their way home in the cabinet, Saburou told Shiina what Erika and the others had told him at the cafeteria.

"Oh," Shiina said. "That explains Tatsuya's behavior the other day."

She knew as much about the Youth Council as Saburou did. Or as the main family worded it—Saburou knew as much Shiina. Saburou's knowledge only came from listening to the eldest Mitsuya son explaining the meeting to his siblings, which included Shiina.

"Then I don't blame him," she said.

"What do you mean?" Saburou asked. He didn't understand how she came to this conclusion.

"Well, clearly, Tatsuya didn't want to put his beloved fiancée in harm's way," Shiina said, matter-of-factly. "That's completely normal."

"But as a member of the Ten Master Clans, don't you think making that kind of sacrifice is a necessary contribution..." Saburou paused, seeing Shiina's mood starting to sour. But he had come this far, so he finished his sentence: "...to magic society?"

"Unbelievable, Saburou. That's disgusting." Shiina's sharp tongue, which she only revealed in front of her childhood friend, came out in the cramped car.

"D-disgusting?"

"Do you really think we should put up with being made a spectacle of just because we're members of the Ten Master Clans?" Shiina bristled. "You're acting like a reporter who says idols deserve to have their privacy invaded."

"Those kinds of reporters don't even exist anymore," Saburou defended. "Anyone who talks like that now would be arrested. Besides, aren't most idols nowadays just 3D avatars anyway?"

"Even avatar idols have real voice actors," Shiina asserted. "And just because entertainment journalists don't say it out loud anymore doesn't mean they don't still feel that way deep down."

She glared at Saburou, dangerously on the verge of pouting.

"But enough about journalists and reporters," she continued. "That's beside the point."

You're the one who brought them up, Saburou thought. But he wasn't about to be counterproductive by pointing that out.

Instead, he said, "But no one at the Youth Council meeting asked Miyuki to sacrifice her personal life. I think Tatsuya's response was kind of extreme."

"I disagree," Shiina said. "If I were him, I wouldn't want my girlfriend running around like a promo model."

"A promo model?" Saburou said with a furrowed brow. "It's not like the council members were asking her to wear swimsuits or miniskirts."

"Maybe not at first. But I'm sure it would just be a matter of time. Miyuki is a beautiful girl, you know?"

Shiina tilted her head and coyly looked into Saburou's eyes. "Don't tell me you wouldn't like to see her in a tight suit top, miniskirt, and either her bare legs or a pair of sheer stockings peeping out underneath."

Saburou fell silent, unable to say no.

"Gross," Shiina spat.

"You're the one who put the idea in my head," Saburou mumbled weakly. It was the best retort he could muster under Shiina's withering gaze.

"The very idea of using Miyuki for advertising tries to thrust both

her magic power and feminine charm into the limelight," she continued, unfazed. "At that point, it becomes impossible to decline any kind of media request. With Miyuki's looks, some of those requests will of course be sexual. I would actually be surprised if they weren't."

"Not all men are perverts," Saburou defended.

"And yet you still imagined her in that miniskirt, didn't you?"

Saburou felt extremely uncomfortable. Shiina's question was a difficult one to answer in general. The fact that Shiina was both beautiful and a childhood friend who knew him well made it almost impossible.

It was too embarrassing to say yes, and even if he said no, Shiina would immediately detect his lie. In other words, she was right on the mark.

She continued. "I think the council members should ask for volunteers. Not force the job on someone just because they're a member of the Ten Master Clans. Besides, it doesn't feel fair to use the pressure of a large group instead of asking in private. Am I wrong?"

"No, I don't think so," Saburou replied.

Shiina wasn't trying to put him on the spot, but he felt increasingly uncomfortable.

"I don't want to speak ill of Mayumi's brother," Shiina said, "but I think Tatsuya's reaction was completely understandable."

If she had said this at the beginning of the conversation, Saburou would have been taken aback. But at this point, he felt his childhood friend may have a point.

[3]

Two days had passed since the Youth Council. Yakumo finished his early morning training with Tatsuya and called out to his disciple.

"Yes, Master?" Tatsuya answered.

"There is mischief afoot," Yakumo said.

"What do you mean?"

"The military's Intelligence Department is on the move."

"Really?" Tatsuya couldn't hide his surprise.

The fact that the Intelligence Department was up to something wasn't particularly out of the ordinary. Plotting was their job.

Yakumo's awareness of their activities was certainly unusual, but it wasn't anything to write home about. Tatsuya had often encountered situations that made him believe his master was more skilled than the entire Intelligence Department combined.

What shocked him the most was that Yakumo's warning was so specific.

"Intelligence's plans don't involve you directly," Yakumo continued. "But sooner or later, the effects will find their way to you."

"I don't suppose you can tell me what these plans are," Tatsuya said.

"What I can say is, if you make a move, the situation will get worse. You may stop the incident itself, but it will not be to your benefit in the long run."

"Okay. I'll stay out of it, then," Tatsuya immediately replied.

Yakumo's lips twisted into a devious grin. "I will tell you about the plans."

"You will?"

"Better to prepare yourself early," Yakumo explained. "That way, you can take appropriate measures in the future."

With that, he pulled Tatsuya to the back of the main hall.

Things turned sour that night in Makuhari New City.

The Japanese branch of Maximillian Devices, a USNA manufacturer of magic engineering equipment, was attacked.

Only a few of the buildings on the premises were in operation, but the factory was not unoccupied. This particular factory was built at the adamant request of the USNA military as a base of operations.

Warrant officer Silvia Mercury was at this secret USNA military base on this night. Silvia was a planet-class member of the Stars, a unit of magicians under the direct control of the USNA's Joint Chiefs of Staff. Her codename also included the word First—a title indicating the highest rank among those of the same planetary rank. Currently, she was fighting with all her might against the despair eating away at her mind.

"All surveillance cameras have gone silent," a base staff member reported.

"It's no use," another added. "The jamming device is too strong. We can't even get in contact with the USNA base."

"There's no way that strong a jamming device was used so close to a metropolitan area," the base commander said. "Unless... Could the Japanese military be involved?!"

With one ear to this conversation, Silvia tried to make sense of the situation by relying on her special magic—or as some people called it, her superpower.

"This is Charlie Leader! Half of the squad's been wiped out! Calling for backup!"

"This is HQ. We read you loud and clear. Bravo Leader, any chance you can help Charlie?"

"HQ, Bravo Leader here. Unfortunately, we're in a pickle ourselves. Not sure if we can make it to Charlie."

Silvia's special ability was called Transvoice and consisted of two spells. One was Clear Audience, which recognized the vibrations in the air produced by a target's voice as information, copied that information, and reproduced it within Silvia's ear canal. This allowed her to hear a target's voice regardless of distance or obstacles, much like a long-distance listening device capable of both communication and eavesdropping. The other spell was Distance Talk, which sensed Silvia's own voice as information, copied that information, and sent it to a target's ear canal.

When she operated these two spells simultaneously, Silvia's ability allowed her to communicate with others even when radio communications were jammed. This evening, she was helping coordinate the magician units that had been dispatched to deal with the attack.

"All right. Delta, can you provide Charlie with backup?"

"Delta Leader here! We need help on our end, too! Who the hell are—? Aah!"

"Delta Leader! What happened? Delta Leader!"

The situation on the battlefield looked grim. It didn't help that everyone chosen for this mission didn't specialize in combat.

The Stars' satellite class, whose members were classified as combat personnel, and the soldiers participating in this mission were usually selected for asymmetric warfare in urban areas. They were not suited for defensive battles where they had to face their targets head-on.

Furthermore, the planet class, of which Silvia was a part, was more apt at logistical support and sabotage missions. Especially compared with stellar and satellite classes, they were not considered skilled at direct combat at all.

On the other hand, it was clear that the magicians attacking the base all excelled in melee combat. The magic they used was not process oriented, emphasizing speed over power. The weapons they carried were small caliber PDWs or carbines. An absence of the telltale crack of gunfire was probably a result of high-performance suppressors acting in concert with sound dampening magic. It could even be CAD-integrated weapons.

Not many of the attackers were fighting with swords or throwing knives. Perhaps because of their proximity to the city, they seemed to specialize in shock tactics.

"Everyone, prepare to retreat," the commander bitterly announced to the base. No one, including Silvia, disagreed with his judgment.

Unfortunately, the decision came too late. Just as staff members followed emergency procedure and erased the base's data with the press of a button, the supposedly locked door screeched open.

"No, it can't—?!"

It wasn't clear if the person who exclaimed was the first commander or second. But Silvia knew the feelings that accompanied that sort of scream.

High-power rifles were manufactured without much thought to cost and durability as they were purpose-built to pierce magician barriers. They were effective weapons that could render the barrels nearly useless after a single battle but were powerful enough to justify their high cost. Even among the Stars personnel, only first-class soldiers could consistently defend against high-powered rifles. Even second-class soldiers could be killed by a non-magician shooter if not adequately prepared.

And yet all of the attackers managed to defend themselves against the Stars' high-powered rifles. This meant that, at least in terms of defense, they were a group of combat magicians on par with first-class Star-level magicians.

It was common knowledge around the world that the Japanese

army had more than enough competent magicians. Lina had warned—even threatened—Sylvia of this prior to the operation.

Still, Sylvia couldn't help but feel surprised.

Did they deploy a special elite force of troops in response to a simple reconnaissance mission? she wondered. *Or is this common practice in the Japanese military?*

In the short time she stood frozen in place, her escort unit was completely wiped out. All units that had been sent out to intercept the enemy had also been completely silenced.

A young female soldier with a carbine passed the line of raiders that held Sylvia's group at gunpoint. Upon closer inspection, she was a noncommissioned officer. A sergeant, based on her rank insignia, which—unlike the other attackers—she didn't bother hiding.

"I'm Sergeant Tsukasa Tooyama," she announced. "A member of the National Defense Force's Capital Counterintelligence Unit in the Intelligence Department. Who is your commanding officer?"

A man stepped forward. "That would be me—Lieutenant Gary Jupiter, member of the USNA Special Operation Command Magician Group, the Stars."

Tsukasa's eyes widened with mild surprise. It was common knowledge in Japan that the code name Jupiter was only given to magicians recognized for their high magic abilities and military achievements.

"I'm sure someone of your stature is already aware," Tsukasa said. "Further combat is pointless. Please surrender."

Gary gritted his teeth in frustration. But he knew without Tsukasa telling him that he no longer had the power to resist. His options were limited.

"Can you guarantee the safety of my soldiers?" he asked.

"Don't you see you are all currently offenders of the law?" Tsukasa said. "You are in no position to demand protection as prisoners of war."

Gary tried to argue, but Tsukasa was faster.

"That said," she continued, "we have no intention of harming service members of an allied nation. We even used nonlethal rounds."

"May I confirm that?" Gary asked.

"Be my guest."

Gary gave the order to the command post staff to confirm the condition of the nearest unconscious guards. Sylvia checked the pulse of the soldier lying closest to her and examined his wounds. As Tsukasa said, no one was injured beyond a bruised and swollen spot where they'd been hit.

"Are you satisfied, Lieutentant?" Tsukasa asked.

"Yes."

"Then we will take all of you into custody for the time being. But don't worry. As long as you do not engage in hostile acts and try to escape, we promise to return you to your home country in the near future."

Gary was puzzled by Tsukasa's obvious condition of not engaging in hostile acts, but he was afraid of how she may react if he asked.

Instead, he simply said, "We appreciate your gracious hospitality." And peacefully relinquished his weapons.

◇ ◇ ◇

The Stars headquarters heard of the infiltration and fall of the Makuhari base approximately three hours later. As soon as the news reached Lina's ears, she stormed to the commander's office and knocked on his door.

"Commander, it's Major Sirius," she announced.

"Come in," he replied. Although Lina had not made an appointment, the base commander immediately allowed her into his office. She saluted him as she entered the room.

"Sir, I—"

Lina trailed off. To her surprise, Colonel Walker was not alone. Colonel Balance was seated at his side.

"How can I help you, Major?" Walker asked.

"...Right." She took a deep breath to organize her thoughts before continuing. "I heard one of our Tokyo bases was attacked."

"That's correct," Walter said quickly, his answer overlapping with Lina's words.

"The entire unit must have been taken captive," she said.

"That has not been confirmed yet," Walter corrected. "All we know is that there were no bodies found."

Lina angrily gritted her teeth. She knew there was no guarantee of survivors just because there were no bodies at the scene. Yet a part of her wanted to believe that Silvia and the others were safe.

"As long as no bodies found, we should assume they are all alive," she said.

"Perhaps," Walker mulled. "Anything else?"

This was her chance. Lina took a deep breath and spoke again.

"I would like to lead a rescue mission."

"Are you telling me that you, the commander of all the Stars, personally want go to Japan and rescue POWs?" Walker asked, enunciating each word slowly.

"Yes, sir," Lina replied without hesitation.

"I'm sorry, but we can't allow that."

This time it wasn't Walker, but Balance, who answered.

"But Colonel!"

"You make a rescue mission sound easy," Balance continued. "But we don't even know where our people are."

"I never said it was going to be easy!" Lina countered.

"Then were you planning to stay in Japan for an extended period of time? You of all people should know that's not possible."

Balance's cold stare was enough to make Lina falter, but she quickly mustered the courage to speak again.

"In order to bring everyone back safely, I promise not to take long."

"So how do you suggest finding where they are being held?" Walker asked. "We don't know the identity of our enemy."

"I will procure assistance when I arrive on site," Lina asserted.

This took a lot of courage to say. Worst case scenario, Lina's claim could be interpreted as a treasonous claim that she had accomplices in the Japanese government or armed forces. But she needed to take this risk if she wanted to save Silvia.

"I never knew you had friends in Japan," Walker said.

"I met a high-ranking *ninjutsu* user on my last mission," Lina explained. "We were enemies at first, but we parted on good terms."

"Is this the Reverend Yakumo you mentioned in your report?"

"Yes, sir."

"How will you get him to help you?" Walker asked, puzzled. "Monetary compensation is the usual option. But you described him as a recluse who has abandoned such worldly things."

"I—"

Balance suddenly stood up and walked right up to Lina. "Even if you manage to convince this Reverend Yakumo to help you, we still can't just fly you abroad, Major. Last year's mission was a special exception."

"...Right."

"Relax," Balance said, placing a hand on Lina's shoulder. The warmth from her palm felt genuine. "The Stars are military personnel who report directly to high command. We would never abandon our own. We will rescue them. In fact, I came to meet with the general staff for that very reason."

Deep down, Lina thought bitterly: *No matter how many hundreds of meetings we have here in New Mexico, we can't rescue Silvia hundreds of miles across the Pacific.*

However, she knew she couldn't say this. There was no choice but to back down.

"Thank you," she replied curtly.

At that moment, Tatsuya's words suddenly echoed in her mind.

"Lina, if you ever want to leave the Stars... If you ever want to quit being a soldier, I think I can help."

It was the night they killed the parasites together. Tatsuya had spoken as if Lina wanted to end her career as a soldier. It was almost as if he didn't think she was *suited* to be one.

This was a very distinct memory of hers. She just didn't understand why she was remembering it now.

[4]

The Magic University stood out for its distinctive curriculum, but its campus life wasn't much different from other universities. In fact, its affiliated magic high schools were much more unique in terms of environment.

In the afternoon, the university's cafeteria was crowded with students who had breaks between classes. Rather than fashion or food, most of their conversations were focused on magic. Yet the mood was still lively. The students body was made up of magicians living in uncertain times, but there was no reason why they couldn't enjoy their youth as long as they had some freedom.

Of course, not all of the students in the cafeteria were having lively debates and conversations. Some were quietly reading, while others were lost in thought. Katsuto was one of the quieter ones, sitting alone with his worries.

"Hi, Juumonji. Mind if I join you?"

It usually wasn't very noteworthy when other students called out to their more soft-spoken schoolmates. But the head of the Juumonji clan, who exuded an air of gravitas befitting his position, was an exception. The only person who dared to impose upon him was Mayumi Saegusa.

"Hello, Saegusa," he replied. "Be my guest. Take a seat."

"Thanks."

Mayumi plopped down in front of Katsuto with no sign of reserve. This was why there were rampant rumors about the imminent engagement between the Juumonji clan head and the eldest Saegusa daughter. Mayumi hated being the topic of gossip, but she also didn't realize that her own actions fanned the flames.

"You look troubled," she said.

"I'm not," he insisted, shooting her an irritated look.

This was supposed to be a hint not to have this conversation here. Unfortunately, Mayumi didn't catch that.

"I bet it has to do with Sunday's meeting," she said.

Katsuto instinctively glanced around while maintaining a poker face. He didn't want other students to notice he was on high alert.

"Don't worry," Mayumi said. "I put up a sound isolation field."

She clearly didn't understand.

"Saegusa, have you ever heard of lip-reading?" Katsuto asked.

"What's that?" she asked. "A kind of telepathy?"

"Never mind," he sighed. "Let's just not talk about the meeting here."

"Hmm..." Mayumi coyly gazed into Katsuto's eyes, an index finger on her chin. But this didn't make her look juvenile. Flirtatiousness was clearly ingrained into her every gesture.

"Okay," she said with a grin.

Katsuto instinctively put up his guard. That grin meant this conversation was not over yet. And he was right.

"So where can we talk?" Mayumi prompted.

"Do you really have to stick your neck into this?" Katsuto asked.

"Hey, that's not very nice. As one of the bright youths of the Ten Master Clans, I'm technically involved," she insisted.

"Fine," he relented. "Do you know Jackson? The coffee shop in front of the train station?"

"I think so," she replied.

"How about we meet on the second floor at 5:30?"

"Sounds good. I don't want to bother you anymore, so I'll see you later."

Mayumi stood up from her seat. Katsuto suddenly realized she had not even brought a drink with her when she sat down.

On her way home from school, Mayumi stopped by an old-fashioned coffee shop. Its name was read as *Jackson*, but it was written with kanji that meant "a place of silence."

"Funny," Mayumi said. "Its catchphrase is even, 'We welcome those who appreciate silence.' They must really love their quiet time."

"Uh-huh," someone mumbled unenthusiastically.

Mayumi wasn't alone.

"What's wrong, Mari?" she asked. "You seem tired."

"That's because I *am* tired." Mari groaned.

"Oh, come on," Mayumi insisted. "You're too young to be acting so old."

"Well, excuse me!" Mari griped. "Unlike the University of Magic, the Defense Academy requires a lot of physical exertion."

Students at the National Defense Academy—even those training to be strategic magicians in the Special Combat Department—were not exempt from basic training and mock battle drills. Mari was genuinely exhausted by the gauntlet her professors put her through. All she wanted to do right now was go back to her apartment, take a bath, and collapse into bed. Those in the Special Combat Department didn't have to live in dorms, so they were allowed that much luxury.

"Anyway," she said, "let's go inside. Didn't you have something important you wanted to talk about?"

"Right," Mayumi replied, under the impression that her friend just wanted to sit down as soon as possible. This time, she avoided calling anyone old.

Mayumi told the waitress she was meeting someone and was instructed to go upstairs. Apparently, Katsuto was already there.

The second floor had four private rooms, all with closed doors. Just as Mayumi was starting to wonder which room Katsuto was in, the door to the far right slid open.

"Come on in, Saegusa." Katsuto beckoned.

He held the door open for the two girls as they stepped into the room. Inside, there was a single table for four. Mayumi was about to say this wasn't an efficient use of space, until she realized the windows were double paned and the walls and floor were soundproof. This was clearly a space for secret conversations. And it probably cost an additional fee to use.

Katsuto led the girls to the table and sat across from them.

"You brought Watanabe with you?" he sighed. "I don't really want this conversation getting around."

"Oh, can I leave, then?" Mari asked. "I'm only here because Mayumi forced me to come."

She stood up, fully intent on leaving. But Mayumi grabbed her sleeve and forced her back into her seat.

"Don't go yet," Mayumi insisted. "I told you this is important."

Mari reluctantly ordered a coffee with the tabletop console. Mayumi ordered milk tea. Once all the drinks were served and the waitress left, Mayumi turned to Katsuto.

"Let me guess," she said. "You're worried about the whole drama that happened with Tatsuya, aren't you?"

"Yes," he answered, deciding it wasn't worth hiding.

Mari had no idea what they were talking about, but she decided not to ask right away. She was going to get involved at one point or other. It didn't hurt to wait.

Sure enough, Mayumi explained: "I'm not sure if you already know this, Mari, but the young members of the Ten Master Clans had a meeting this past Sunday. Well, I say young, but the cutoff was thirty."

"Yeah, I heard about that meeting," Mari said. "You were discussing what to do about the extremists targeting magicians, right?"

"Our focus wasn't extremists," Katsuto corrected in an irritated

tone. "It was on how we magicians should respond to the increasingly anti-magician climate."

"What's the point of that?" Mari asked bluntly. "We can fight back against criminals, maybe, but you can't force the masses to like us."

Mari was originally part of the Hundred Families, but she lived for the most part outside the mainstream magician community. Her minimal connection to magic society and the magic world meant her values were more in line with the military than with Mayumi and Katsuto.

"You're right. We can't force people," Mayumi conceded. "But we can state our case to them. Don't you think emphasizing our social contributions could help relieve the tension building between magicians and non-magicians?"

"I'm not so sure about that," Mari countered. "If we pressure them too much, it might create resistance."

Just as Mayumi and Mari were spiraling into an endless argument, Katsuto intervened.

"You have a point, Watanabe," he admitted. "But at the recent meeting, many of the members were intrigued by Saegusa's idea."

"Well, it's a fine idea," Mari said. "The problem is what exactly are you going to do to make it a reality? Put Mayumi on TV and make her address the public?"

Mayumi spun to her friend. "What?! Why me?"

"You have a nice face," Mari responded flatly.

"Why are you making it sound like that's my only redeeming quality?" Mayumi pouted.

Once again, Katsuto intervened before the argument could escalate any further.

"The point is," he pressed, "the idea was brought up at the meeting, but it wasn't Mayumi we considered. It was the Yotsuba family heiress."

Mari looked surprised. "You mean, Tatsuya's kid sister? Or should I say, fiancée? Was she not at the meeting herself?"

"No," Katsuto said. "Shiba attended the meeting alone."

"Well, that sounds like a recipe for disaster," she groaned. "There's no way Tatsuya would approve of putting his fiancée in the public eye like that. He's way too overprotective."

"You're right. He didn't approve of the idea," Mayumi said. "In fact, the entire meeting ended on a sour note because of it. To make matters worse, he didn't attend the group luncheon afterward. That earned him the ire of the other attendees."

"He got backlash from *all* the attendees?" Mari asked in disbelief. "Not a single person defended him?"

"Not publicly, no," Katsuto replied.

Mari's face twisted into a sickened scowl.

"That sounds like peer pressure to me. Awful. It's this kind of stuff that makes me think magicians are just like regular human beings."

"We *are* regular human beings," Mayumi said. "The only difference is we can use magic."

Before the conversation could get sidetracked, Katsuto refocused the topic.

"I think both those who tried to use the Yotsuba heiress and Shiba, who was firmly against the idea, have their reasons."

"The problem is," he continued, "the Yotsuba clan may become uncooperative if Shiba is made into a pariah."

"Don't be ridiculous," Mari said. "That would be like a parent interfering in their child's battle."

"Think about it, Mari," Mayumi interjected. "Tatsuya is the Yotsuba hieress's fiancé and the current Yotsuba head's son. What Juumonji is saying is not an understatement."

Mari leaned back against her chair and emitted a big sigh.

"Well, that's upsetting. It's like we're dealing with court politics or something."

"As long as blood ties are important, the magic world is bound to resemble aristocratic society," Mayumi mused. "But I'd like to believe it resembles an ancient city-state led by a hereditary parliament rather than a feudal, class-based society."

"That sounds terrible, if you ask me," Mari countered. "Don't you know ancient city-state societies were built on the backs of slaves?"

"Oh dear," Mayumi said. "Well, we could replace the ancient slaves with automated machines. That makes it less inhumane, right?"

"Saegusa, Watanabe, that's enough." Katsuto interrupted yet another tangential conversation. "If you keep digressing every time you speak, we'll never get anywhere."

The two friends awkwardly hung their heads.

"I'm sorry," Mari mumbled.

"Me too," Mayumi echoed.

Katsuto let out a small sigh. "Anyway, we have to do something about Shiba's current isolation from the other twenty-eight families. The Ten Master Clans are now at the top of the Japanese magic world, but not everyone likes it this way."

"So if the Yotsuba family breaks away from the Ten Master Clans, there might be attempts to create a new faction of Yotsuba supporters. That's what you're most worried about, isn't it?" Mayumi asked Katsuto.

He nodded bitterly. "It isn't as if we can tell either side to apologize. Neither Shiba nor the others have violated any rules. They simply spoke and acted in accordance with the purpose of the meeting."

He turned to Mayumi and Mari.

"Since you're both here, I'd like to know if you have any ideas."

"Let's see..." Mari spoke up first. "If the main problem is that the meeting wasn't very productive, why don't you just hold the meeting again?"

This suggestion caught Katsuto by surprise. He stared at Mari in silence until Mayumi stepped in.

"What would the meeting's purpose be this time?" she asked.

"Well," Mari began, "the last meeting was held to discuss the best way to deal with anti-magicians. Why don't you use the next meeting to discuss those strategies in more detail?"

"But the last meeting ended with opinions sorely divided," Mayumi worried. "I wonder if people will actually come this time."

"Don't you get it? You're holding this one *because* the last meeting ended without any agreement." Mari turned to Katsuto: "You were the moderator at Sunday's meeting, right?"

"Yes." He nodded.

"Was the meeting supposed to decide upon a specific strategy then and there?"

"No. It was my first time doing this sort of thing, so I just wanted to create an open forum to share our thoughts."

"Then the true purpose of the meeting was to encourage young thinkers to share their ideas," Mari clarified. "At the very least, the attendees should have been aware of this hidden agenda and acted accordingly, right?"

"Yes, I guess they did," Mayumi said with a sigh, remembering her brother's unfortunate lack of tact.

"What I'd like to know is how anyone could propose using the Yotsuba heiress under those circumstances. That's like a military staff member suggesting the commander's daughter should be the mascot to promote the base. It's one thing if she wants to do it. But if the proposal is made without the daughter's consent, that staffer is headed straight for a demotion. People like that really need to learn how to read a room."

Although Mari's metaphor was based on military custom, both Mayumi and Katsuto understood what she was trying to say.

"Then again," she continued, "Tatsuya needs to learn how to read a room, too. The Yotsuba clan is more than capable of declining a proposal to use their heiress at a later time. Tatsuya didn't need to resist the proposal so strongly right then and there. It's that naïveté of his that convinces me he's still a child."

"Are we talking about the same person?" Mari's statement felt so strange that Mayumi couldn't help but pose the question.

"Actually," Katsuto said, "I think Shiba resisted the proposal on purpose. It was almost as if he was using it as an opportunity to side with the Yotsuba family and express that he doesn't care what the other twenty-seven families think."

"Interesting," Mari mused. "Well, it will be meaningless—counterproductive even—if Tatsuya doesn't show up at the next meeting."

Katsuto fell into thought. The best option would be to get Tatsuya to compromise. He just couldn't think of a good premise or method to get him to do so.

"Why don't the three of us try to convince him?" Mayumi suggested, as if reading Katsuto's mind.

"You mean *us*?" Mari asked.

"Sure," Mayumi said. "We could ask Tatsuya to compromise as a favor to help Juumonji save face. I'm sure he would say yes."

"Do you really need me there, though?" Mari groaned.

"Of course we do." Mayumi pouted. "You're my friend."

"But I'm not even part of the twenty-eight families."

Mari's tone was more one of hesitation than refusal. Mayumi clung to her.

"Come on, don't say that. There's no way I could mediate a conversation between Juumonji and Tatsuya all by myself…"

"Here we go," Mari sighed, a hand to her forehead. "Fine. I'm already involved, so I might as well see this through. Are you fine with that, Juumonji?"

Juumonji paused, not sure what she meant by "that." But Mari continued before he could speak.

"The meeting's poor ending doesn't make the Juumonji family look very good. I don't know about Tatsuya, but the other attendees are probably concerned."

"Oh!" Mayumi said. "That means if Juumonji himself sends out an invitation to another meeting, the other clans will have no choice but to comply."

"Right. In the meantime, the three of us will try to persuade Tatsuya to accept a compromise. Actually, if possible, Mayumi and I will use Juumonji's name as a ticket to talk to Tatsuya and his fiancée together."

"You want to talk to Miyuki, too?" Mayumi gasped.

"Yeah, his fiancée is... Agh, I just can't get used to calling her that," Mari said. "But Shiba's former kid sister *is* the cause of all this tension. Not to mention the focal figure in this mess. Plus, I have a feeling Tatsuya will be more mature—calmer even—when Miyuki is around."

"Good point. Is it okay if I'm the one who reaches out to Tatsuya?" Mayumi asked.

"Sure," he replied.

"Make the meeting on a Saturday, if you can," Mari said. "Weekdays are hard for me."

"Why not a Sunday?" Mayumi asked in a teasing tone.

"I leave for field exercises next Sunday."

"Wow. Your life is tough," Mayumi said sympathetically.

"Thanks to you guys," Mari retorted, eliciting an awkward laugh from both Mayumi and Katsuto.

[5]

Apart from her required magician's education from the magic high school, Miyuki took various lessons in etiquette. These lessons included Japanese and Western manners, dancing, flower arrangement, and tea ceremony. While this may seem like a lot, Miyuki's excellent memory helped her master most of it by the time she graduated from junior high. Now in her final year of high school, she only attended a finishing school for young upper-class ladies once a week.

The day of the week these lessons fell on was not fixed. While this system was slightly unusual, it helped the school's students avoid becoming a target of kidnapping. Miyuki herself didn't have to worry about that, but it was helpful for the school's non-magician students who couldn't fight.

"Take care of her, Minami," Tatsuya said when he dropped the two girls off at the school.

"Don't worry. I would risk my life for Miyuki," Minami reassured.

Boys were not allowed on school grounds. That meant Tatsuya wasn't even permitted to escort Miyuki to her classes. In the past, he would entrust her to the school's security guard at the entrance. But once Minami joined them, he left Miyuki in her capable hands.

Miyuki had long planned to stop attending the school before summer so that she had time to study for the Magic University entrance exam. But with the current situation growing increasingly tense, she considered moving up her end date.

After leaving the two girls at the school gate, Tatsuya began his usual routine of killing time at a random coffee shop until Miyuki's lesson was over.

He tended to stay away from casual dining restaurants because of some trouble he had caused during the vampire incident. Of course, there were other places he could wait. But he was afraid that—sooner or later—he would exhaust all of the places in the vicinity.

Tatsuya paid his bill at an automated register and left the shop with more than half a cup of coffee left. He didn't want to get the establishment involved in any trouble that might be following him around. Last time, no windows were broken, no customers were injured, and no other real damages occurred. He intended to keep it that way and make sure the only ones who had to deal with the aftermath were himself and his opponent.

The signs that danger was near were very similar to last time. If Yakumo hadn't divulged the details about the situation in advance, Tatsuya may have been caught by surprise.

Why, he wondered, *are American magicians attacking me again?*

"*The deserters have joined Target A.*"

"Continue monitoring. Have all civilians been guided to safety?"

"*Affirmative. No civilians in the AO.*"

A quiet smile spread across Tsukasa Tooyama's lips as she listened to the conversation between her supervisor and the on-site personnel. So far, so good. The operation was going according to plan.

The puppet control is proceeding smoothly, as well, Tsukasa thought. *It's a pity the puppetry technique wasn't applied to the satellite class. Then again, it does seem to be easier to replicate, so no skin off my nose.*

Tsukasa was the brains behind this operation. The supervisor in command here was a second lieutenant, but it was Tsukasa—although only ranked sergeant—who really held the reins. This unexpected command authority was thanks to the powerful influence she held over the head of the Intelligence Department as a result of a secret agreement between the National Defense Force and the Tooyama family.

Tsukasa was intentionally re-creating the situation that took place a year prior in February—the situation where Lina attacked Tatsuya with Brionac. Tsukasa's aim was to make Tatsuya think history was repeating itself. And so far, it was working.

We don't have Naotsugu Chiba to help us this time, but the powerful pawn Angie Sirius isn't around either, Tsukasa mused. *That means, the game might play out more or less the same. Either way, I'm looking forward to seeing what you'll do, young Yotsuba.*

She continued to wait calmly with a smile pasted on her lips.

Twenty enemies, all of them…unarmed. Well, that's strange.

Tatsuya was analyzing his surrounding enemies via the information body dimension, Idea.

They look like the same kind of Stardust members as last year, but for some reason, the Idea is showing some strange static noise.

He sensed familiar eidos bodies on the verge of snapping. At the same time, there was unfamiliar static, which seemed to be traces of psions from an outside source.

It's like Gu Jie's corpse-controlling magic, but these enemies aren't corpses, Tatsuya thought. *I wouldn't call this mind control, either. It's as if their cerebrums were surgically or medically manipulated to take away their free will. Ancient magic commands are being used to control their behavior.*

"Now, this is unfortunate," he murmured.

I wanted to send them home unharmed, but it looks like that's not an option.

Yakumo had given Tatsuya two pieces of information. The first was that the National Defense Force's Intelligence Department was about to attack a USNA military unit that had infiltrated the Tokyo suburbs. The second was that the very same Intelligence Department was planning to use captured USNA soldiers to attack him and Miyuki. What Yakumo didn't divulge was why they were interfering with the Shibas' lives. Or what they wanted to know.

Tatsuya didn't try to force this out of his master. That kind of information was impossible to know. The fact that he even knew they were planning to attack felt like cheating. Then again, fairness didn't apply to this kind of test, so Tatsuya didn't feel bad in that respect.

He decided to walk toward a busy street. It wasn't that he wanted to involve civilians; he just wanted to harass whoever his attackers were.

As soon as he left the coffee shop, he noticed the streets were decidedly empty. Whoever was behind this must have fabricated some kind of construction project or accident to control the flow of traffic. Clearly, even the Intelligence Department was hesitant to involve the public. It also meant that if Tatsuya headed toward a busy area, they would try to attack before he could get there. He was determined to derail his enemy's plans by expediting their attack.

Is my enemy really the National Defense Force's Intelligence Department like Yakumo said? Tatsuya pondered. *Or was it all a lie?*

The answer to these questions was more important to him than the impending battle itself.

"Target A seems to be headed toward a busy zone," one analyst warned. "Sir, at this rate, we may not be able to adequately isolate the civilian population."

"...Fine," the commander said reluctantly. "Send the puppets in!"

Tsukasa, who was simply observing the operation, felt a tinge of unease. Things were deviating from her original plan. The dice that had been so secure in her palm were now on the verge of slipping through her fingers.

At the same time, she felt it worth pressing forward. She knew now, at least, that Tatsuya Shiba was not an idealist who felt the need to protect civilians at all costs.

"The puppets have encountered Target A," an operator announced. "Operation moving to phase two."

The USNA soldiers launched an attack on Target A, aka Tatsuya. Deprived of their free will via the ancient magic puppetry technique, the Stardust unit became the pawns of Tsukasa's operation. The unit was made up of magician soldiers who had not been chosen to directly be part of the Stars but volunteered to undergo enhancements and abandon their so-called normal human status. Now even their wills had been altered, and they attacked Tatsuya on command.

You're not going to use any flying techniques? Tsukasa thought, directing her silent question at Tatsuya.

Observing the scene from street camera footage, she was mildly surprised that Tatsuya did not use long-distance magic to intercept his opponents.

Even though Tatsuya was more physically fit than the average Japanese person, most of his USNA attackers were taller and more muscular. Combined with the fact that he was outnumbered, it was expected for him to attack from a distance to avoid close combat.

A thought suddenly passed through Tsukasa's mind: *He must know we're watching him.*

The possibility was not low enough to be completely off the table. It made sense that a magician accustomed to using magic illegally in the city would develop an awareness of when he was being watched. There was no scientific evidence for this, of course, but a series of similar cases naturally raised doubts. At the very least, Tsukasa certainly suspected it.

She deduced to herself again: *Although there was no record in the Intelligence Department's database, we can probably conclude that Tatsuya Shiba has long been involved in the Yotsuba family's illegal activities.*

Meanwhile, a battle had begun between Tatsuya and the Stardust soldiers-turned-puppets on a street clear of bystanders.

One of the puppets swung a large knife, aiming for the tendon in Tatsuya's arm. In order to take advantage of their large numbers, a common tactic was to degrade their opponent's ability to fight.

The Intelligence Department did not give the puppets firearms to avoid the risk of stray bullets hitting something unfortunate. If there were no other means of attack on both sides, the battle would have inevitably devolved into hand-to-hand combat involving knives, blunt weapons, and fists. However, both Tatsuya and the Stardust soldiers were magicians. The soldiers did not lose their magic just because they became puppets. They could still cast spells from a distance. This was the kind of battle Tsukasa and the rest of the Intelligence Department anticipated.

Ultimately, the first attack still involved a knife. But the puppet used magic to accelerate his movements.

Tatsuya dodged and suddenly appeared behind his attacker. Even Tsukasa, watching the street camera footage, couldn't tell how he got there. If the puppet had any humanlike will left, he would have been astonished.

Tatsuya used his hand to strike his opponent in the neck. The puppet's body dramatically collapsed. Tsukasa's eyes darted to the psion sensor monitor attached to the street camera. No magic was detected.

So he can cast spells without triggering psion sensors, she thought, bemused.

It was usually impossible to stun someone with a karate chop to the neck. Not unless someone hit hard enough to leave a terrible bruise or used a special technique.

Tsukasa thought a high school student from the Yotsuba family was much more likely to have the ability to deceive sensors than to render someone unconscious with a single blow.

Unfazed by the sight of his comrade going down, another soldier lunged at Tatsuya. Simply turning the soldiers into puppets didn't make them fearless. The puppetry technique Tsukasa used only stripped the soldiers of their free will and imprinted new commands. This could erase loyalty and a sense of belonging, but it could not erase fear—a necessary mental function for self-preservation. The soldiers' lack of fear stemmed from the fact that both their bodies and minds had been altered when they joined the Stardust.

Tsukasa didn't think anything of this. She similarly used magic to turn people into puppets, and brainwashing people to do their bidding was common practice in her line of work.

It was for another reason that she raised a brow.

The monitor displayed Tatsuya, one against twelve, or at this point, one against nine. But despite his overwhelming disadvantage, he sent the brainwashed soldiers to the ground one after another.

"Captain," an operation personnel called out, "at this rate, Target A will be finished fighting before the other unit can make contact with Target B!"

The operator seemed to have noticed the same thing Tsukasa had. A February ago, the USNA military had tried unsuccessfully to capture Tatsuya with a Stardust unit plus a magician presumed to be Angie Sirius. Aware of this, the Intelligence Department did not believe that Tsukasa or anyone else could defeat Tatsuya with Stardust alone.

The puppets' role at this stage was to stall Tatsuya. The main mission had not yet begun. Tsukasa's objective was to gather information on Tatsuya, but that, too, was still in its initial phase. The first stage may have seemed to be the perfect opportunity to acquire data on Tatsuya's fighting abilities, but Tsukasa was more interested in something else.

"Expedite the attack against Target B," the commander ordered.

Just then, the four remaining USNA soldiers simultaneously fell to the ground.

"The puppets have been wiped out," personnel reported. "Target A has left the stage."

Tsukasa was impressed. The psion sensors didn't detect Tatsuya's magic from beginning to end.

Miyuki's etiquette lessons catered to young ladies from well-to-do households. Put more bluntly, they were girls with upper-crust families who could afford the school's high monthly tuition.

As was common for such schools, its security was very strict. In fact, they employed guards capable enough that even a crime syndicate wouldn't test them. This was why even parents with dark secrets were willing to accept the outdated no boys policy and entrust their daughters to the school.

However, that night, the school's illusion of safety came crashing down.

"Everyone please stay calm!"

An instructor, seeming more panicked than her students, shouted over a high-pitched alarm.

"We must follow the emergency procedures and evacuate to the safe room! You will be safe there. Now please move quickly and calmly!"

Ironically, she was the one who needed to calm down the most.

The number of students differed every day, but there were ten this night. All of them whispered to their personal hired escort. Only one student other than Miyuki was a magician, but all the escorts were magicians. Other than Minami, all the escorts were in their twenties to early thirties. They all seemed more dependable than the instructor.

"What do you propose we do, Miyuki?" Minami asked.

"At this point, I can only foresee a future of us cowering in the safe room." Miyuki smiled regrettably. "It would cause problems for the school if we were to run off and do our own thing. Let's be good and follow what the instructor says for now. You can always bar the safe room entrance if needed. It should be easy enough to wait until Tatsuya comes to get us, right?"

"As you wish," Minami said.

Miyuki's decision was quick. She called out to a couple of nearby students and said, "Let's be off," before leading the way to the safe room without waiting for a reply. Minami hurried close behind while the group of students and their escorts followed.

As far as Miyuki could tell, the school guards were putting up a decent fight. The only element holding them back was that the other side was much better.

Minami supported the guards' efforts with a shield in the connecting passageway to block a series of electric attacks. It was only after the blasts stopped that it became clear they were caused not by electricity sparks but ultrathin, airborne wires spiked with electric currents.

"Nice work, Minami," Miyuki commended. "I'm impressed."

"Thank you."

Miyuki praised Minami's foresight to block the attacks with a physical barrier, rather than an anti-electricity one. Discerning the nature of the enemy's magic and executing the appropriate defensive technique in a matter of seconds was different than simply performing a high level of magic. Minami's accomplishment gathered glances of conviction and astonishment from the magicians in the room.

The astonishment came from the fact that Minami's high magic proficiency was beyond her years. The conviction came from the fact that such a magician was entrusted to guard the Yotsuba family heiress, who was worthy of the best.

Meanwhile, the other young ladies' escorts didn't just sit back and do nothing. The trespassers were not only attacking head-on. The straight pathway prevented any attacks from the side, but there were several attacks coming from both ends of the hall.

Miyuki turned her attention to the tail end of the group, where a pair of women in their twenties years were suppressing the attacks to their rear.

"I wonder who those two fighting in the back are," she said. "They don't look familiar. Do you know them, Minami?"

"Apparently, the girl's name is Tsunashima," Minami said. "Her escort is Tsunaga."

"Tsunashima and Tsunaga?" Miyuki echoed. "Strange. Those names don't ring a bell."

Although not quite as good as Tatsuya's, Miyuki also had an exceptional memory. It was unlikely she would forget a classmate's name, much less if that classmate was a magician who belonged to one of the Hundred Families.

"Tsunaga said they joined the school recently," Minami explained.

"I see," Miyuki said. "It's a shame they have to deal with an incident like this not long after they started."

Despite the calm nature of their conversation, the two girls were running down the hall while fending off attacks from the intruders. The other young ladies were close behind.

With Minami and Miyuki battling at the front, Tsunashima and Tsunaga battling at the back, and the other students plus their escorts and the instructors following in the middle, the group finally arrived at the safe room.

Once most of the group had made it inside, Minami and Miyuki stayed by the door, waiting for Tsunashima and Tsunaga, who were still fighting. They weren't necessarily trying to follow the principle of *noblesse oblige* or anything—Miyuki was simply the strongest person present. She could easily overpower both the escorts and trespassers.

Minami pulled a portable terminal-type CAD from her pouch and offered it to Miyuki. Up until now, Miyuki had been using a fully thought-operated CAD, undetectable by third parties.

She accepted the familiar CAD with a smile, turned it on, and began typing on its surface. In a matter of seconds, she aimed at a pair of dark men about to attack the group and sent them flying backward. The time lag between the spell's input and attack was barely perceptible.

Tsunashima became paralyzed with wonder at Miyuki's display of power, but Tsunaga was quick to urge her forward. They finally made it into the safe room.

Suddenly, a new group of assailants appeared at the other end of the hallway.

How many of them are there? Miyuki frowned and began operating her CAD again.

Brass-colored rings around the trespassers' fingers glistened under the hallway lights. They were using cast jamming.

"Miyuki!"

Minami ran to the rescue, a small but solid combat knife in her hand.

"It's all right," Miyuki calmly soothed her scowling defender. "This is the perfect opportunity to try out the new spells Tatsuya made me."

The two large male trespassers fearlessly ran forward. Facing them head-on, Miyuki quickly activated her CAD and cast two consecutive spells.

For a split second, it was as if the psion noise froze. It didn't literally freeze over; it just fell silent. Miyuki winced as she dropped to the floor, too shocked to break her fall. Minami's eyes widened like saucers.

It wasn't the instant neutralization of their enemies that surprised them. It was the spell's ability to put an end to the psion noise that rendered them speechless.

Cast jamming was the most effective means of magic interference currently in common use. It used the rare man-made mineral thought to be a relic of prehistoric civilization called antinite. Anyone who possessed antinite could almost certainly interfere with magic activation, even if they themselves couldn't use magic. It was, therefore, the most powerful weapon a non-magician had against a magician. But Miyuki just demonstrated that cast jamming could be blocked.

"The anti-magic, Freeze Program. This is the spell my brother—I mean, my fiancé, made for me," she gushed breathlessly. "It doesn't nullify all magic like Program Demolition or Program Dispersion, but it's enough to counteract cast jamming."

Although she hid it well, Miyuki was over the moon.

Freeze Program was an enhanced version of area interference. Magic that it could nullify included typeless magic, area-of-effect magic, and any spells that were in the process of activation. It couldn't erase magic with a specific target, but it could completely nullify cast jamming, a typeless magic variant, as Miyuki demonstrated.

"There are probably no more than ten…no, eight more intruders left," Miyuki noted.

"I think you're right," her Minami confirmed.

"Then let's leave the rest to the guards and await Tatsuya's arrival."

"All right."

Miyuki and Minami entered the safe room. Miyuki took a seat on one of the sofas placed far from the wall. Minami stood in front of the locked door, ready to activate barrier magic at a moment's notice.

Tatsuya arrived at the finishing school less than ten minutes after the girls were attacked and about five minutes after Miyuki entered the safe room.

No one had informed him about the attack. The school's communication in the event of a trespasser was usually flawless—unless, as was the case this time, the Intelligence Department was involved.

Tatsuya did not go to the school because Yakumo told him Miyuki was a target. Nor was it because he realized the attack on him had been a diversion. He was simply there because his top priority was always to ensure Miyuki's safety.

The fighting had ended by the time he arrived, but from the look of things, there had clearly been a violent case of breaking and entering. Still, Tatsuya remained calm. Even without confirming it with his own eyes, he knew Miyuki was safe because of their close bond.

Tatsuya could even tell where she was by turning his attention to the information provided by his Elemental Sight. Using a special technique, he read the signs of multiple intruders within a ten-meter radius. The accuracy of the former tool was far better than the latter, but it was impossible to misread the signs in a situation where all parties were in clear view.

Ignoring the no boys policy, Tatsuya entered the trampled school grounds without batting an eye.

Not everything has gone according to plan, but now it's time for the finale.

Tsukasa worked herself up as she watched the footage from the etiquette school's hacked surveillance cameras. This time, she had sent in both a unit of USNA Stardust soldiers-turned-puppets and her own subordinates.

Tsukasa faced a constant, distorted experience of seeing herself from a third party perspective. Since she was only allowed a shadow of an identity, she tended to neglect even what was necessary to stay alive, like eating and sleeping. Such was the price the Tooyama family paid in exchange for power.

"Commander," Tsukasa said.

"Yes, Sergeant Major?" he replied.

"The operation is starting soon. May I be excused?" she asked.

The second lieutenant frowned quizzically before remembering what his superior had told him when he had been assigned this mission—do whatever Tooyama asked.

"Permission granted," he said.

He would much rather have Tsukasa gone than making outrageous demands that countermanded his commands. Taking her request as a blessing, he decided to get rid of her as soon as possible.

"Thank you," she replied.

It wasn't clear whether Tsukasa knew the second lieutenant considered her a nuisance. A cryptic expression crossed her face as she saluted and left the room.

Tatsuya didn't know Miyuki was hiding in a safe room. He figured that's the sort of place where she must be, but he couldn't relax yet. He headed toward her location without even a glance at the guards collapsed on the hallway floor.

Once there, he encountered enemies. Some of the intruders who had attacked the school were trying to pry open the sturdy doors of the safe room.

Tatsuya flew into action without a sound, not jumping but gliding toward the intruders. They noticed Tatsuya just before he reached them. But, since they were under a form of mind control, they didn't panic. They simply switched their attention from the door to Tatsuya, wielding their Stardust skills.

Before they could even activate their magic, Tatsuya released a few psion bullets he had been clutching in his right palm. He had not yet mastered the technique of wielding armor-piercing psion shells when USNA forces first attacked him in February. Originally developed to damage parasites, the technique was now often used for attacking psions present within the human body. These bullets were so effective that they even worked on Hagane Tomitsuka, who had psion armor strong enough to repel magic. Tatsuya's Stardust targets, who didn't boast half the psionic density as Tomitsuka, tumbled backward like they'd been struck in the chest by a large-caliber bullet.

Psions had no physical striking power, but they were interconnected in a way that mirrored the structure of human and animal bodies. This made it possible for the wielder to manipulate the psionic system and move at a speed faster than the nervous system's reaction time.

Tatsuya shot out pressurized psion shells one after the other. To those who could see psions, it would have appeared as if he were launching glowing spheres of energy from his palms.

When psions struck a person, the human psyche commanded the body to reproduce a level of damage it expected to feel after sustaining an attack. There was a similar typeless magic technique called Phantom Blow. The reason why Tatsuya chose to neutralize his opponents with armor-piercing psion shells instead of annihilating them with Dismantle was to create the illusion of using Phantom Blow.

This roundabout fighting style was meant to deceive anyone who might be watching. Tatsuya concluded that if the military was involved, it was safe to assume the surveillance cameras in the school had been hacked.

Without Yakumo's warning about this attack and his attacker, Tatsuya would have disposed of his targets more quickly. There was no other reason to go to the trouble of making it look like a proper fight. Having grown tired just before encountering the intruders, Tatsuya decided to switch from direct combat to psion shells. As long as the National Defense Force's intentions were unclear, he didn't want to reveal how much he knew.

There had been eight intruders in front of the safe room door. Once Tatsuya was done with them, they were all lying on the floor, unconscious. He had put an end to the battle without suffering a single hit. If his enemy had been equipped with guns, they would have caused him more trouble. All of a sudden, Tatsuya paused.

USNA magicians had a preference for CAD-integrated weapons. These were purpose-built to include CADs, providing magically enhanced attack power while still allowing the user to access the weapon's special functions. Apparently, USNA magicians favored combining CADs with firearms. In fact, the Stardust's first move during their raid the previous year was an attack with sub machine guns that had integrated CADs.

But if they like guns so much, why aren't they carrying them now? Tatsuya wondered.

Providing firearms would have been easy enough if the National Defense Force and Intelligence Department were involved. Besides, these Stardust soldiers were simply disposable, brainwashed foreign agents. Even if the police found out about the guns, the National Defense Force could have easily feigned ignorance.

It was almost as if Tatsuya's opponent was trying not to put up too much of a fight.

Feeling like he had been lured into a trap, he was suddenly sick to his stomach. But it was too early to know what was going on. He had no other choice but to take things in stride.

Figuring Miyuki and the others were observing the situation from a surveillance monitor inside the safe room, he waited for them to open the door.

Tatsuya had eliminated all of the puppets. Tsukasa confirmed this in a room separate from the command center. But no surveillance cameras were installed in the safe room, so she couldn't tell what the Yotsuba heiress and her escort were doing while they were inside. Now that the intruders were eliminated, Tsukasa assumed the girls would open the door and come out. That would be her chance. She checked the magic line between her room and the others.

The connection was good.

She may have used ancient magic to turn the Stardust soldiers into puppets, but she was not by nature a user of unorthodox magic that interfered with the human psyche. She was a Tooyama family magician from Lab Ten. That meant she had been bestowed with area magic to create virtual constructs, specifically magical barriers.

Even if she established a magic link between herself and another person, Tsukasa could not use that link to read minds. Nor could she relay perception information or directly manipulate the will of another person. All she could do was tell where someone was, identifying the coordinates of her target based on the information dimension.

But that was more than enough for a member of the Tooyama family. If they needed material information, such as sound or visuals, they could use a remote device. The Intelligence Department's spy equipment wasn't weak enough that a few obstructions or jamming would render it useless.

Knowing a target's information dimension coordinates was the key to activating their magic. That sort of thing could not be accessed with electronic devices. There were rumors about magicians and magic support systems that could link visual information to information dimension coordinates. But Tsukasa had doubts about rumors like that.

The targeting assistance systems of specialized CADs were designed to enhance information within the range of its user's own senses. Someone who possessed Elemental Sight, which directly observed the information dimension, may be able to determine target coordinates based purely on information data. But there were limits to this ability. The tangible maximum distance that humans could perceive, for example. Infinite expanses only existed as abstract concepts. Herself aside, Tsukasa believed nobody should be capable of focusing their consciousness on specific information bodies (eidos) within the information dimension (Idea) as they would have to be deeply broken people to even stand a chance at such a feat.

It wasn't inconvenient for her to think this way. The magic bestowed upon the Tooyama family and the role Tsukasa had been assigned did not require technology that aimed at targets in extremely remote locations via visual information alone. Nor was it required for the current mission at hand.

She focused her attention on the images from the hacked surveillance cameras to support her loyal subordinates.

An antique door fixed with an ornate doorknob slid open in front of Tatsuya. He couldn't help but crack a smile at the playful disguise. This was why no matter how much the trespassers had pushed and pulled, the door wouldn't budge.

Minami stood just beyond the door. She greeted him, bowing politely. Miyuki walked up to him with a graceful stride. The only reason she didn't rush to his side was because she was wary of strangers' eyes.

"Thank you for coming in my time of need," she said.

As far as Tatsuya could tell, Miyuki hadn't been in much danger, but he chalked it up as the normal thing to say in situations like this.

"I'm glad you weren't hurt," he said.

"Thanks to your quick rescue," she replied.

This was not a formality, but how Miyuki truly felt. It was a given in her mind that Tatsuya would come to her rescue. And yet actually seeing his face filled her with joy. Above all, she was relieved that Tatsuya's arrival was much earlier than expected. She failed to hide all those emotions and anyone paying attention could see how she was feeling.

The everyone else in the room stayed frozen. Not because they were frightened, but because the sickly sweet atmosphere made it difficult to move. The first to break free from the spell was the other magician pair who had been fighting at the rear.

"Apologies for the delay. I'd also like to thank you for coming, Shiba," the younger lady said.

For some reason, her polite language seemed awkward, almost theatrical.

"My name is Tsunashima and this is Tsunaga," she said. Then turning to her escort, she urged, "Come, you must thank him, too."

Tsunaga came forward between Tsunashima and Miyuki. Tatsuya's body instantly moved from stationary to top speed, his hands pushing Tsunaga away. Tsunaga, who had tried to restrain Miyuki with an arm around her neck, fell limp to the ground.

"Don't move!" Tsunashima yelled.

At the same time, Tatsuya cried, "Minami!"

Tsunashima grabbed a random student and held a concealed knife to her neck. Minami reacted to Tatsuya's signal by protectively shifting herself in front of Miyuki.

Tsunashima began, "Move and this innocent girl's life is—"

But Tatsuya turned away before she could finish, unleashing a spell at Tsunaga—Miyuki's attacker. Miyuki and Minami were not the only ones who heard the phantom smash of shattering glass. It was the sound of a magic barrier breaking.

Tsunaga had put up a barrier as she was falling, and Tatsuya's magic disintegrated it. He didn't dare to show it, but Tatsuya felt a growing sense of unease. When he had pushed Tsunaga, it was not only his hands that made contact. First, he used disintegration magic from his palm to instantly dissipate the magic shock wave that Tsunaga had deployed. Then, he channeled a small but high-pressure psion current into his strike.

This completely dispelled the barrier magic. But his psion current should have also made it impossible for Tsunaga to construct magic properly for a good while. The psions of other magicians were magical foreign substances. While psion currents within the human body and the subconscious magic-calculation region were separate, they were not entirely independent. Rather, they were connected within a common network which was what made it possible for the activation sequence output from a CAD to be entered into the magic-calculation region via the body. If someone else's foreign psions were injected into this network, they made magic activation impossible for at least a short period of time.

And yet Tsunaga, who couldn't even stand back up, had somehow deployed a magical barrier. Chronologically speaking, this could only have happened *after* Tatsuya infused psions into his strike. Just because she was physically paralyzed didn't necessarily mean she couldn't use magic. But this was not something a magician of her caliber should be capable of.

Tatsuya didn't pause while he was puzzling through these conundrums. With his right hand raised, he unleashed a carefully compressed psion current toward the fallen Tsunaga.

Program Demolition.

Originally designed to dispel magic programs, this spell achieved a similar effect to infusing psions on contact by increasing the psion current's permeability.

Tsunaga's frame convulsed once and stopped moving altogether. She seemed to have lost consciousness. If Tatsuya had hit her hard on the head or put pressure on her heart, there was a possibility that she could have died. He used Program Demolition as an enhanced remote attack to avoid the hassle of cleaning up that sort of aftermath. Luckily, it apparently worked as intended.

Now it was time to deal with Tsunashima.

Blood flowed from her hostage's neck. Not a great big fountain, just a trickle. Tsunashima had only let her blade sink in a tiny bit. Her ability to exert the perfect amount of force to do this suggested that, contrary to appearances, she was either experienced or professionally trained. Unfortunately, her actions were in vain.

Miyuki was the only one who made sense to use as a hostage here. Even if Tsunashima had put Minami's life on the line, Tatsuya would have prioritized neutralizing his enemy over ensuring her safety.

Of course, Minami was perfectly capable of fighting off most enemies herself. And if Miyuki was taken as a hostage, she would freeze her captor into a block of ice unless they possessed some mystical treasure that nullified magic. Long story short, using hostages against Tatsuya was not the wisest choice.

Tatsuya prepared to fire a psion bullet at the magician who

claimed to be Tsunashima. Just then, he noticed that a magical barrier had formed around both her and her hostage. Tatsuya couldn't hide his surprise. The strangest part was that there were no signs that Tsunashima had activated the barrier magic. She also didn't have the skills needed to completely conceal her activation of magic.

Then where is it coming from? Tatsuya thought.

Someone else was clearly deploying a magical barrier around her. There was no other possible explanation. In an instant, Tatsuya destroyed the magic barrier. Then he used his left hand to reach for Tsunashima's knife. The blade crumbled into powder in the palm of his hand. The breakdown of both the barrier and the knife were caused by Tatsuya's disintegration magic.

His lingering concerns did little to hinder him on the battlefield.

He grabbed Tsunashima's right wrist and twisted it outward. She didn't resist, instead kicking off the floor to perform a somersault through the air. Tatsuya then released Tsunashima's hand, pulled the hostage toward himself, and passed the her back to Minami. She caught the hostage just before the poor girl staggered and fell.

As soon as Tsunashima touched back down, Tatsuya delivered a side kick. Right on cue, a magical barrier came up. Right as Tatsuya's foot was about to make contact with the barrier, it shattered. Controlling his magic and body separately, he kicked Tsunashima in the chest. Unlike with Tsunaga, he didn't hold back. Tsunashima's heart stopped as she suffered sudden cardiac arrest.

Tatsuya struck the magician in the chest with lightning at the same time her body crumpled to the floor. The flash cast magic delivered a weak electrical shock that miraculously served as a defibrillator, and the girl's heart began beating again.

Seated on a hard-cushioned chair, Tsukasa opened the single eyelid that she had been keeping closed. Her magic worked just fine with

both eyes open. But she felt it was more precise when she blocked a few of her senses. When delivering magic from afar, she always chose to close one eye.

"So he won't hold back even when going up against women," she mused.

Tsukasa was in her private room. Taking advantage of the fact that no one could hear her, she openly talked to herself.

"I'm surprised he shattered my magic barrier so quickly. Of course, it wasn't as strong as usual, since I wasn't using it as it's meant to be used. But at this rate, I'm going to lose faith in my own skills."

She shook her head with the usual fake smile plastered on her lips.

"No. What am I thinking? I shouldn't expect anything less from a Yotsuba magician. But I am curious about the spell he used to shatter my barrier. It was almost as if he broke the magic program itself. Did he use Program Dispersion?"

Tsukasa shook her head again, this time with a scoff at the very thought.

"Impossible. That spell only works in lab conditions. It's not practical for actual combat."

At this point, it sounded like she was having a conversation with someone else.

"On a separate note, it seems even a Yotsuba magician can't neutralize magic in standby mode. Then again, if he could affect me at such a distance, he wouldn't be considered a magician anymore, now would he? Such power could only belong to someone superhuman. Or a monster."

She turned both eyes to the surveillance footage. Tatsuya was crouched by Tsunashima's side. The camera in the school hallway was aimed at the inside of the safe room, but all it could capture was Tatsuya's back, and it wasn't clear what he was doing.

"There is no place in this country for superhumans. If you are truly a monster, you have my sympathies. But that simply means you must disappear."

She whispered to the boy's image on the monitor in a voice an oblivious bystander may even call gentle. The reality was anything but.

Asking Tatsuya to leave was not an option. In Tsukasa's mind, he had to be destroyed.

Tatsuya crouched beside the magician he had defeated, searching for traces of magic. She had not been the one who cast the magic barrier. The only thing he could be sure of was that the magician who did cast it wasn't in this building.

The culprit was clearly capable of incredibly precise remote magic. One possibility was that Tsunashima had been acting as a relay point for this magic. The technique of using a person as a magical relay was rare but not unheard of. Just a couple of months ago, Tatsuya had witnessed a magician working with Gu Jie use ancient magic to turn a young man into a relay point to perform SB magic.

As it stood, Tsunashima wasn't emitting any magic identification signals. Even Tatsuya's enhanced eyesight couldn't detect anything.

Did the culprit use visual information to determine the coordinates in the information dimension? he wondered.

Technically, this was possible. Tatsuya's Third Eye similarly used images from platforms in the stratosphere and Low Earth Orbit Satellites to assist its aim. It probably wasn't a coincidence that Tatsuya could sense someone observing him through nearby surveillance cameras.

The magic that deployed the barrier...unfortunately can't be traced, he thought. *The residuals are too scant.*

Tatsuya's Elemental Sight wasn't perfect. On top of that, it was difficult to investigate the identity of an agent that had been carefully crafted to not leave any trace of information. It might be possible if Tatsuya put in 100 percent effort, but it was unfeasible under the current circumstances.

"Tatsuya?"

Miyuki called out, her voice tinged with apprehension. She must have been concerned by the troubled look on his face.

"No need to worry," Tatsuya replied. "It looks like everything has been taken care of here."

He stood up with a smile. Miyuki smiled back. Then he called out to the other member of their household.

"Minami."

"Yes?"

Minami had just finished returning the hostage to her original escort. She stepped forward now just behind Miyuki when she heard her name.

"I need you to call the police. And take care of Miyuki while I check the area for injured people," Tatsuya ordered.

"Yes, sir," Minami replied.

"I'll be right back, Miyuki."

"Of course," she said. "Please be careful."

She gave him a dignified bow, cautious not to instinctively treat him like her elder brother.

[6]

It was Saturday, April 20, after school.

On this day, the First High student council room was missing both its president and secretary general.

Miyuki had informed the other officers two days earlier that she and Tatsuya would be absent from the daily student council meeting. The reason behind this was Mayumi's invitation to meet, delivered on Wednesday night.

Miyuki didn't tell Honoka or Izumi about Mayumi's invitation. As Mayumi's sister, Izumi might have known about it already. Then again, for all anyone knew, the topic of the planned discussion could be top-secret, so Miyuki simply said that she had business to attend to.

Honoka had not yet arrived at the office. The only ones present were Izumi, Shiina, and the public morals committee member—aka an outsider—Kasumi. Miyuki had proposed to give everyone the day off, but Izumi insisted she could take care of it. And so the daily meeting's attendees were reduced to a select few. Naturally, Minami was not one of them, since she was off accompanying Miyuki.

Kasumi, Izumi, and Shiina had been friends since childhood. Now that the three of them were alone, the student council room was bathed in a relaxed, almost languid atmosphere. Nevertheless, Izumi was diligently sorting through the various clubs' activity reports for recruitment week. Shiina was helping her. And Kasumi was relaxing with a cup of coffee.

"Izumi?" Kasumi sat sidewise with one elbow on the table and spoke to her sister's back.

"What is it, Kasumi?" Izumi replied without turning around or stopping her pen.

"Do you think president Shiba's absence today has to do with that thing?"

"What thing?"

Even though they were twins, this kind of telepathy wasn't their strong point.

"Remember how Mayumi said she was going out today? Maybe she went to meet up with the president and Tatsuya."

Having reached a stopping point, Izumi suddenly stopped what she was doing and rose from her chair.

"It's a possibility," she said, taking a seat next to her sister. "Pixie, can I have some tea, please?"

Pixie stood up from her own chair in the corner of the room with a brief "Right away."

"On the other hand," Izumi continued, "it could be a complete coincidence. Thank you."

She took a cup of green tea from the 3H robot. Izumi could drink both green and black tea, but she preferred Western sweets and Japanese teas.

"Mayumi may look like a social butterfly, but she sticks around people she knows more often than not."

"Ha! She's such a cat," Kasumi said, taking a sip of her black coffee with no sugar. She tended to have mature tastes when it came to coffee.

"She is," Izumi replied. Then to herself: *And you're like a puppy.*

It was fun to tease her sister, but she decided to hold herself back around Shiina to avoid any chance of causing embarrassment.

"Our student council president doesn't seem to have many friends, either," Kasumi noted.

"That's because Miyuki is a goddess incarnate," Izumi stated matter-of-factly. "Solitude suits her."

Kasumi cringed and muttered "Wow…" under her breath, but Izumi didn't seem to care. In fact, she pitied her sister. It was unfortunate Kasumi couldn't understand how amazing Miyuki was. Shiina, meanwhile, gazed on at the two in confusion.

"Why don't you take a break with us, Shiina?" Kasumi suggested.

"Yes, please join us," Izumi echoed.

"All right," the younger girl said.

Shiina sat across the table from the twins, a cup of milk tea with plenty of honey in hand. She had the biggest sweet tooth. And yet her homemade sweets were never overly sweet. Preferences were strange in that way.

"So," Kasumi began again, "why do you think our catlike sister and goddess-like president could be meeting today?"

"Remember how Mayumi said she was going to a restaurant in Akasaka?" Izumi said.

"Not really…" Kasumi scratched her head.

"Well, she did." Izumi sighed. "But of course you don't remember. You always only pay attention to things that interest you."

"I wasn't not interested!" Kasumi said defensively. "Are you sure I was even there?"

Now that only her friends were around, Kasumi's speech patterns started to reflect her usual rough way of speaking.

"Who knows?" her sister replied.

"What's that supposed to mean?" Kasumi asked.

"Well, *I* for one directly asked Mayumi where she was going today," Izumi said. "Your mind must have been somewhere else."

Kasumi gritted her teeth in frustration, sensing her sister's condescending tone. But she couldn't get herself out of this one. Izumi was probably right.

"Anyway," Shiina jumped in to stop an impending argument, "the question on the table is why Mayumi wants to meet with the president and Shiba."

Izumi compliantly softened her tone. "Maybe she wanted to talk about the Youth Council."

"You mean the one last Sunday?" Shiina asked.

"Yes," Izumi nodded. "Mayumi mentioned Katsuto would be at the restaurant, too, so they probably either want to scold or placate Shiba for his wild behavior at the meeting."

"I don't know if we should call it 'wild,'" Kasumi intervened.

"All right," Izumi admitted. "I guess that's unfair of me to say."

"Do you have something against Shiba?" Kasumi asked.

"I never thought *you* would be asking *me* about that," Izumi said in mock surprise. "You're the one always glaring daggers at him."

"I don't glare daggers!" Kasumi said defensively. "I just don't like him very much."

Isn't that basically the same thing? Izumi thought.

"I heard that!" Kasumi shouted. "And you're wrong!"

Even though Izumi had not said her thoughts aloud, Kasumi spoke to her as if she had. Her reaction was too perfect to be a coincidence. Knowing what the other was going to say before she said it was definitely a twin thing.

"It's all right," Izumi said. "Shiba bothers me sometimes, too."

But I'm probably the only one conscious of how we feel, she thought.

This gave her a strange sense of superiority over her sister. But she tucked it away to avoid making Kasumi defensive again.

"I appreciate how much he treasures Miyuki," she continued, "but he never tries to help anyone else even though he can. And he has a high level of insight but never bothers to check in on how people are feeling. Shiba is the most heartless guy I know."

"You're…not wrong," her sister replied hesitantly.

Tatsuya was not in the same room, but Kasumi still found her twin's lack of tact when talking about their senior at school a little shocking.

"I have noticed that Shiba has a lot of skills," Shiina agreed. She was not interested in Tatsuya romantically, but she was curious about him as a member of the same student council.

"I can also see that he has incredible insight," she continued. "He just doesn't seem to have empathy."

"In other words," Kasumi clarified, "he may *know* how someone feels, but he can't *understand* those feelings."

"Of course I couldn't hold it against him if that were the case." Izumi sighed. "But I think Shiba has the ability to analyze feelings."

"Analyze?" Shiina questioned. "Not empathize with?"

"Yes, analyze," Izumi repeated. "And yet he ignores those feelings if he deems them superfluous."

"I think you're taking this too far…" Kasumi began.

"No, I am just stating facts. Shiba may look handsome and composed on the outside, but he is cold-blooded on the inside when it comes to anything other than Miyuki."

Kasumi was again taken aback by her sister's forwardness. Shiina, on the other hand, put both hands to her cheeks, which for some reason had flushed pink.

"Um, Shiina?" Kasumi ventured. "Why do you look like a flustered schoolgirl?"

"I just think Shiba and Miyuki's relationship is wonderful," Shiina gushed. "It's straight out of a fairy tale."

"Say what?" Kasumi said, afraid she had heard wrong.

"I mean, Shiba practically lives for Miyuki, and Miyuki alone," Shiina explained. "Wouldn't you love it if a man gave his entire heart and soul to you?"

"Uh, I don't know," Kasumi replied hesitantly. "That sounds like a lot of pressure."

"Oh, Kasumi, you're just too nonchalant when it comes to romance," Shiina said.

Me? Nonchalant? Kasumi wondered.

Kasumi? Nonchalant? her twin echoed internally.

Then, aloud, Izumi said, "Maybe we're just not romantic enough to understand. Anyway, let's get back to what we were talking about originally."

"Oh, right." Kasumi shook her head. Clearly, neither of the twins was as starry-eyed as Shiina.

Izumi continued. "I was out of line before about Shiba, but I do think Mayumi wants to talk to Shiba and Miyuki about the future."

"Yeah," Kasumi agreed. "Katsuto definitely seemed to be worried about Shiba's behavior at the youth council. Mayumi must be trying to fix things in her usual meddling way."

"I wonder what she is planning," the younger twin wondered. "Since Shiba is involved, I doubt she would spontaneously jump into a conversation and risk an argument."

"Maybe she's going into this knowing it might turn into a fight," the older twin offered. "I doubt Shiba would be willing to listen to anything she might say, though."

"You might be right. Katsuto, on the other hand, is a different story. He is head of the Juumonji, after all."

"I agree Shiba will listen to him, but I don't think Katsuto's position matters. The Juumonji's poster girl idea probably won't go over well, either. The Yotsuba family is powerful enough to hold their own without associating with the Ten Master Clans. If Shiba has been influenced by Yotsuba ideas, compromise will be off the table."

"Right again. I, for one, would love to see Miyuki on TV, but… all things considered, using the Yotsuba family heiress as a poster girl is a ridiculous idea. I'm sure Tomokazu knows what the Yotsuba are capable of if he makes them angry."

"But our brother doesn't get Shiba at all. That's why he didn't think his idea to make Miyuki appear on TV was a big deal. If only Katsuto had stopped him. On second thought, that would've been impossible."

"Right. Katsuto has always been this way."

The twins exchanged wry smiles that Shiina didn't quite understand. The younger girl didn't know Katsuto like they did.

"Aw, man," Kasumi said anxiously. "Now I'm getting worried. I really hope they don't set off another land mine."

"Don't say that. There are no land mines to set off," Izumi insisted, but her face was pale with fear.

"Hey, you know where they went, right?" Kasumi asked her twin. "Why don't we go see what's happening for ourselves?"

Izumi shook her head. "There's nothing we can do."

Yet there was a hint of uncertainty in her voice. Shiina sensed it.

"Maybe not," Kasumi said.

"But should we still go?" Izumi asked.

"Hmm…"

Shiina looked on in silence as the twins stared into each other's eyes, pondering what they should do. The silence was only broken by the arrival of a visitor. Rather than use the regular entrance, Honoka and Shizuku entered the student council room from the stairs.

"Good work today, you three," Honoka said with a generous smile.

Shizuku, on the other hand, had a slight frown on her face. "What are you doing, Kasumi?"

"Kitayama!" Kasumi exclaimed, scrambling to her feet and freezing in place. "We weren't slacking off, I swear!"

"Right," Shizuku answered. The tension between them was so thick you could cut it with a knife. "Don't worry. I heard you were off duty. I was just wondering why you and your sister were staring at each other."

The tension finally eased, and Kasumi breathed a sigh of relief.

"So what's going on?" Shizuku insisted. "Were you enthralled by your identical faces?"

"N-no!" Kasumi immediately denied.

"How could you think that? We're not narcisissts!" Izumi added, also rising to her feet.

"Narcissus? Like yuri?" Shizuku said in a way that made it hard to tell whether she was playing dumb or being serious.

"No!" Kasumi exclaimed.

"Also, narcissus is a daffodil, not a lily!" Izumi added.

Shizuku glanced away coldly from the heated Saegusa sisters and turned to Pixie to check the facts.

"Daffodils were classified. As part of the lily family. In the old Cronquist system. Today, they are classified. As part of the amaryllis family," Pixie reported instantaneously from her database.

"Oops, I was wrong," Shizuku said sluggishly. "Pixie, can I have a cup of tea?"

"Right away," the 3H robot replied.

Shizuku plopped down at the table as if nothing had happened, while the twins melted exhausted into their chairs. The plan to sneak into Mayumi's meeting was instantly put to rest.

While the twins were slumped over in their seats, the other three girls leisurely sipped their warm drinks. Just then, Pixie walked over to Shiina's side.

"Shiina. You have. A guest," she announced.

"A guest?" Shiina quickly activated her terminal and checked her school email. Sure enough, she had a message announcing the guest's arrival.

"Thank you, Pixie," she said. Then, turning to the others, "Mitsui, Izumi, it seems I have to leave. Is that all right?"

"Sure," Honoka said. Izumi didn't say anything different, so Shiina nodded.

"Thank you. Pixie, could you take care of my cup?"

"Right away."

Shiina walked to the office door and spun around.

"I'll see you later," she said with a bow, and exited the room.

Her bag with all of her belongings was left behind.

◇ ◇ ◇

A vast training forest lay behind First High School. It was a place where students could practice magic without disturbing the surrounding residential area, so spaciousness was key. The area included an undulating terrain formed by artificial hills, an open-air swimming pool, and an extensive waterway.

A boy was making his way across a wooded, cross-country course with poor visibility. He wasn't just running. Sometimes, he would turn back as he ran. At other times, he pulled over to the edge of the path to hide behind a grove of trees.

The boy was Saburou Yaguruma, a current freshman at First High. He was running away from a group of people. But his pursuers weren't terrorists or thugs, like those who raided First High before.

The mountaineering club was helping with Saburou's training at Erika's request. The ten club members, including Leo, were now chasing after the long-haired boy as he tried to escape.

Saburou had to run a total of five kilometers to successfully evade his pursuers. He was allowed to follow any path, even if that meant leaving the road behind and weaving through the woods. The club members each held a toy knife and if any of them managed to touch him, the chase would to start all over again.

These were the conditions Erika imposed. When Saburou first heard them, he was optimistic. All he had to do was avoid the toy knives. Even if his pursuers caught up with him, he would have no problem fending off a knife and escaping when he saw his chance. He soon realized, however, that this was easier said than done.

First of all, his pursuers had more than one knife. Even though they were amateurs, dodging their persistant attacks was no walk in the park. To make things worse, more pursuers would gather if he took too long to escape. Once Leo caught up, it also became difficult to handle the attacks themselves.

Leo learned to handle a sword before the Yokohama Incident in under a month's time. Now he was an expert in close combat, one of the best Saburou had ever met.

Many active-duty military personnel frequented Lab Three. Saburou been practicing with them since childhood, thanks to the Mitsuya family's connections. Although his magic skills never improved significantly, he had gained recognition from the military personnel, who claimed his combat skills were on par with the National Defense Force's assault teams. As a result, Saburou was confident that he had grown stronger.

After entering First High, though, he was reminded that there was always someone better. He didn't stand a chance against Erika, and Aizu, the head of the *kenjutsu* club, always seemed to have the upper hand. When the club's vice president, Yayoi Saitou, was roped into the match, she launched Saburou into the air with a move apparently called Tora-giri. She was unexpectedly powerful for her size. Even though he was wearing protective gear, the moment he was hit, he sincerely thought, *So this is how I die.*

Then there was Leonhard Saijou. When the two boys first met in the dojo, Saburou thought he was strong, but nothing to write home about. His first impression was that Leo was the type of fighter who dominated his opponent with power, stamina, and feral instincts rather than skill.

This impression remained more or less unchanged. But Saburou realized from their first round in the mountains that Leo's true potential was not on a matted floor, but outdoors. And he was viscerally reminded that Leo's real strength was not in his bamboo sword but in his arms and legs.

I can't get caught. I have to get out of here.

Saburou realized this on his third attempt. Now he was already on his sixth.

He had run nearly ten kilometers in total. All of his original pursuers had been replaced by new members, except for Leo. If he couldn't get away this round, he knew he would collapse.

Saburou's ears picked up the steady sound of someone approaching from behind. He ran off-course and into the woods. The footsteps belonged to Leo. Even though both boys had been running for the same amount of time, the older boy's footsteps didn't reveal the slightest sign of exhaustion. Saburou shuddered at Leo's inexhaustible stamina and silently moved deeper into the woods.

"Found you!" Leo shouted from behind.

Damn! Saburou thought and picked up the pace.

Leo's yell was mostly meant to flush Saburou out. Whether he had actually found Saburou was questionable. But the younger boy fell for the trick, forgetting the importance of stealth.

He heard footsteps flying over the undergrowth. Now he had really been found. Abandoning any attempt to remain hidden, he bounded ahead as fast as his legs could carry him.

A few minutes later, Saburou was sprawled out in a clearing that the mountaineering club considered their turf. In the end, he was unable to finish the race before running out of steam.

"You okay?" Leo plopped down next to the younger boy with a trace of concern in his voice.

"...Yes," Saburou wheezed between gasps for air.

"You didn't earn yourself a gold star, but that wasn't bad at all," Erika praised. "I'm surprised you held out so long against these high-stamina beasts."

None of the mountaineering club members resented this tasteless nickname. Even Leo laughed it off. They were clearly aware of their endurance.

The mountaineering club members weren't the only ones who ignored Erika's comment.

"Don't get too close, Shibata. It's dangerous," one art club member warned.

"You probably won't get hurt with all that water, but you don't want your sketchbook to get wet," another art club member added.

They were talking to Mizuki, who had been making sketches. She heeded the club members' words and stepped away from the edge of the hole she was peering into.

At its deepest point, this massive hole was five meters from the water's surface. It was Leo's handiwork after becoming the new head of the mountaineering club and attaining the student council's permission. Its purpose was to form a cliff for climbing.

Under Leo's supervision, the mountaineering club had recently shifted its emphasis from fitness, survival, and pickaxing to activities better suited to its name. Free climbing was one of these new activities. Club members who did not participate in Saburou's game of tag were happily tackling the rocky overhang. There were no climbing ropes or harnesses, but a heated pool three meters deep with temperature of 30 degrees Celsius was installed at the bottom of the cliff. Even if someone fell, they would only get wet. Of course, there was always the chance that their clothes would get heavy with moisture, their soggy shoes would slip, and they would get stuck in an endless loop of climbing and falling. But the ladders in place made it possible to escape.

The art club was currently working on a project called Muscles in Motion, which revealed a portion of the members' personal tastes. Mizuki had chosen free climbing as the subject for her sketches. At first, she let out an adorable shriek every time a mountaineering club member fell, but she got used to it after about an hour. Now she was happily sketching one of the climbers working his way up the cliff as he dripped with sweat.

Leo stood up to try out the wall himself when a voice called out to him from the forest.

"Leo."

Mikihiko stepped out of the trees in a practically immaculate school uniform, compelling the mountaineering club to break into awestruck whispers.

"Only a guy like that could be Leo's friend," one member gushed.

"Leave it to the disciplinary committee president to break the laws of common sense," another praised quietly.

Leo ignored these comments.

"Hey, Mikihiko," he greeted. "I never see you around these parts."

"I heard a student fainted, so I came to check it out," Mikihiko replied. He glanced at Saburou, still lying on the ground. "But it looks like everything is fine."

All the mountaineering club members held back the urge to shout, *"What about him looks fine?!"* Clearly Saburou was not doing well, but the club could be written up for misconduct if the school found out what they were putting him through. They decided to keep quiet, and Saburou didn't object.

Erika called out to him. "Can you stand?"

"…Yes," he replied, pushing himself to his feet. He was still very unstable but willed himself to stay upright.

"Yoshida, why don't you help him out with his training?" Erika said.

"Me? Are you sure?" Mikihiko stammered, caught off guard.

"Please," Erika insisted.

"Well, all right," he relented. "I can't use magic, though."

"That's fine," she said.

It wasn't that Mikihiko was unable to use magic. He simply meant that, as the disciplinary committee president, he couldn't violate the school's policy on the unauthorized use of magic. Luckily, Erika seemed okay with that. She turned to the long-haired boy.

"Saburou, just so you know, even without his magic, Yoshida is one of the best students at this school. Don't try to win. This is just a chance to learn something."

"Got it. Yoshida, I'm ready when you are," Saburou said, shifting into a defensive stance.

Mikihiko hesitated for a second before quickly shrugging in defeat. He couldn't back down now. Especially with Erika involved.

As soon as he started unbuttoning his blazer, Mizuki was behind him to take it. Then suddenly, he was directly in Saburou's face.

Saburou instinctively thrust out his arm, but Mikihiko was quick to grab his wrist and fling him to the side. Saburou's body easily soared through the air and fell to the ground. Since Mikihiko was quick to let go, none of Saburou's joints were injured. Realizing this, Saburou quickly got back to his feet, observing his opponent's movements.

"Why didn't you attack me while I was taking off my blazer?" Mikihiko asked, perplexed.

Saburou was suddenly hyperaware of his own naïveté, and it prickled him with regret. Taking advantage of this moment's hesitation, Mikihiko moved closer again on Saburou's right side. He raised his left arm up slowly and rammed his fist into Saburou's chin. The younger boy thudded to the ground. Then the disciplinary committee president pressed his knee to Saburou's chest, seized Saburou's right hand with his left hand, and placed the fingers of his right hand over Saburou's eyelids. Saburou tapped his opponent's knee with his free left hand to signal he gave up. Mikihiko rose to his feet, exposing his back. Saburou saw this as an opportunity to attack from behind, but Mikihiko spun around, avoiding his grasp. Then the older boy pulled the younger boy in, locked his arms behind him, and pinned him down as if riding a horse.

"Amazing!"

Mizuki clapped her hands in delight at Mikihiko's magnificent moves. It had been a while since he displayed them in public.

"Geez…"

Leo, on the other hand, winced like he had just chugged the most bitter drink. Erika wore a similarly sour expression from the combination of Saburou's lackluster performance and Mikihiko's clever fighting style.

"Do you want to keep going?" Mikihiko asked, releasing his hold on the younger boy.

"Please!" Saburou replied without hesitation.

For the next half hour, Saburou spent more time on the ground than on his feet.

◇ ◇ ◇

"Shiina sure is taking a while," Izumi mumbled.

After processing the reports from various clubs, she looked up at the clock, slightly concerned.

"You're right. It's way too long for a simple visit," Kasumi agreed.

She had been working on disciplinary committee work as soon as Shizuku saw she clearly had time on her hands.

"I wonder who came to see her. Do you know, Pixie?" Kasumi turned to the 3H robot as if talking to a human.

"I am sorry. That is private information," Pixie replied in a stereotypical machinelike fashion. Since this kind of routine phrase was easy on the AI, her speech was smooth.

"How can you give me such a mechanical reply?" Kasumi protested with a cynical smile. Needless to say, both she and Izumi knew Pixie was a machine.

"My master. Has instructed me. To act like a machine," Pixie replied in a way that hit both sisters harshly.

"It's bad manners to snoop into someone's email," Shizuku added.

"Right. I'm sorry." Kasumi sighed in defeat.

Her relationship with Shizuku went beyond that of seniority. Shizuku, especially, was keenly aware of this.

It was then Pixie that replied. "That is all right. Miss Mitsuya has already. Left school."

All four girls looked up in surprise.

"When did that happen?!" Honoka demanded.

"Sixteen minutes and fifty seconds. Ago," Pixie instantly replied.

On paper, the 3H robot only had the ability to pass commands to the student council room system. She technically shouldn't have access to this kind of information, like what time a student left campus. But no one in the office gave this a second thought.

"That's strange," Shizuku murmured.

"What's strange?" Honoka asked anxiously.

"She left her things behind."

A look of panic suddenly crossed Kasumi's face, and she jumped to her feet.

"Sorry, everyone," she said. "I need to go."

"Go where?" Izumi pressed.

Even if Kasumi went to ask the main office about Shiina's location, they would probably deny her the information on the grounds of private information. The school faculty would also give the same answer.

"To Saburou. I'm pretty sure the mountaineering club is training him today."

With that, Kasumi raced out of the student council room.

When Kasumi reached Saburou, he was wheezing on his hands and knees. Mikihiko was giving him a concerned look as Mizuki helped him slip back into his blazer. It was a bizarre scene, but Kasumi decided against asking questions. She didn't have time.

"Excuse me, everyone! I need to speak to Saburou!"

She walked directly over to the long-haired boy and—ignoring the dirt that soiled her uniform—got down on her knees to look him straight in the eye.

"Where the heck did Shiina go?" she demanded.

Saburou suddenly forgot to breathe. The color drained from his face—but not from a lack of oxygen.

"Shiina's…gone?" he gasped.

"You didn't know?" Kasumi countered.

Erika, Leo, and Mikihiko gathered around the two, concerned. Just then, Saburou broke into a coughing fit.

"Hey, are you okay?"

Kasumi reached out to him, but he moved away.

"I'm fine," he said, unsteadily getting to his feet. With a wobbly gait, he ran to his bag as fast as he could, removed the communication device from his portable information terminal, and stuffed it into his ear. Forgetting to lower his voice, he shouted into the device.

"Dad! Shiina's gone! Have you heard anything?"

The man on the other end of the line was Saburou's father, Shirou Yaguruma.

"*Shiina?*" Shirou asked. "*Hang on. I'll be right back.*"

He hung up. About a minute later, his name appeared on Saburou's terminal screen.

"This is Saburou. Any news?"

"*It doesn't sound like the Mitsuya clan gave her any specific instructions,*" Shirou said. "*Can you tell me what happened?*"

He didn't criticize his son for losing track of Shiina. In fact, he wasn't even treating Saburou like Shiina's bodyguard. This made the situation all the more painful.

"I just heard about it myself..." Saburou admitted pitifully.

"*All right,*" his father said. "*Motoharu said he will ask the school about it.*"

There was a pause as Shirou spoke to Shiina's elder brother. Then he continued, "*You don't have to do anything. Acting rash without understanding the situation will only make things worse.*"

"...Fine," Saburou said. "Tell me if you learn anything new."

"*I will. It's possible Shiina will return to the school. Wait there for her, will you?*"

"Sure."

Saburou hung up the call, clearly upset. Recognizing he wouldn't be able to think clearly for a while, Erika decided to speak up.

"Kasumi. Tell us what happened," she said.

"Right. Um..." Kasumi hesitated. To tell the truth, she was as much in the dark as everyone else. But she tried her best to tell the group what she knew.

"So someone called her to the conference room..." Erika murmured.

"Wouldn't it be reasonable to suspect whoever that 'someone' was?" Leo blurted.

"We can't say she was kidnapped just yet," Mikihiko insisted. "She might have gone somewhere with the visitor of her own volition. For all we know, she might have even gone home."

Kasumi shook her head at this last conjecture. "She left all her stuff in the student council room."

"Then let's go there," Erika said.

"What good will that do?" Leo protested. "Wouldn't it be better to force the main office to give us information?"

Erika put her hands on her hips. "We're not as powerful as Tatsuya or Juumonji. The main office won't listen to anything we say."

"But why do you want to go to the student council room?" Leo pressed.

"Pixie is there."

A sudden look of realization passed over Leo's face, but this time Kasumi dissented.

"Pixie said she can't give out personal information."

"She will if she knows it's an emergency." Erika smiled. "Her programming is pretty flexible."

"I'm with Erika on this one," Mikihiko chimed in. "Let's go to the student council room."

"Whoa. This might be my first time there," Leo revealed.

"That's surprising. I thought you must have been called in for your behavior at some point," Erika teased. "Oh, wait. That must have been the disciplinary committee."

"They've never called me in, either!" Leo vowed.

What had started simply as an honest comment turned into a joke that helped ease everyone's tension. Just a little.

"Please, Pixie, it's an emergency," Honoka begged. "Can you tell us who Shiina met?"

"I am sorry. I cannot reveal that information. Without my master's approval."

It seemed Pixie refused to answer even Honoka's plea.

Pixie had originally been awakened by a series of thought waves that Honoka inserted. To the mental information body that resided within her, Honoka was her mother—the person who gave her life. Unfortunately, this didn't mean she felt obliged to follow Honoka's orders. Pixie's master and the person she devoted her life to was Tatsuya alone.

When Honoka hung her head in defeat, Shizuku stepped in.

"Pixie," she said. "Your master is away on important business."

"That is. Correct," the robot answered.

"If we called him right now," Shizuku continued, "we would be interrupting whatever he is doing."

"Most. Likely."

"But we will have to call him if you refuse to acknowledge our emergency."

"Cannot. Bother. Master."

"Then please tell us who met with Shiina. We're so worried about her we are prepared to bother Tatsuya, if necessary."

Pixie fell silent.

At this moment, her orders not to divulge private information conflicted with her orders not to bother Tatsuya. If she was your average machine, this conflict of interests might have made her programming freeze. Luckily, the mechanism that ran her system was a consciousness information body called a parasite. This helped her prioritize orders in a way that imitated free will.

"Very well," she said.

The room burst out into exclamations of surprise and delight. As soon as Pixie began speaking again, everyone fell silent.

"The person who met with Shiina. Called herself. The Mitsuya Clan. Angel."

Erika spoke up. "But the Mitsuya family said they didn't know anything about Shiina's disappearance."

Pixie stiffly turned to her and motioned to a large display.

"Please take a look. At this footage."

The school's surveillance camera footage appeared on the screen. This was clear evidence of Pixie's hacking abilities, but no one in the room seemed to care. They were much more worried about the issue at hand.

"This is the woman who. Called herself. The Mitsuya Clan. Angel," Pixie explained.

The footage revealed a man and woman. The woman appeared to be in her early twenties, while the man was probably in his thirties. Despite their age difference, the man was extremely polite to the woman.

"That woman looks familiar," Izumi said slowly.

"They're both in the military," Erika asserted with conviction after a single glance.

"Aren't there a lot of soldiers who use Lab Three?" Mikihiko asked.

"That's true, but..." Kasumi began.

"None of the members of the Mitsuya family are soldiers themselves," Izumi finished.

"So these soldiers just ran off with the Mitsuya girl without telling her family?" Leo asked.

"Congratulations, Leo." Mikihiko smirked. "Your abduction theory is looking more real by the second."

"Miki!" Erika rebuked. "Don't talk like that!"

Mikihiko noticed the pale look on Saburou's face and quickly apologized.

"Sorry."

"The problem is," Leo continued, "it's not normal for soldiers to just spirit away high school girls."

"Unless those two are Lab Three regulars and Shiina knows them," Mikihiko offered.

"But again, the Mitsuya family already said they didn't know anything about Shiina's disapparance," Erika repeated.

"I think we need to keep watching so we're sure she didn't just go home," Honoka said.

"Agreed." Shizuku nodded.

"Good point," Erika said, then turned to the long-haired boy. "Saburou."

The sound of his name made him jump, and he lifted his head.

"You should go home," she ordered. But Saburou shook his head.

"My dad told me to stay here."

"Oh, right. I guess you have to stay until he calls, then." Erika bit her lip in aggravation.

"Anyway, it's a big deal if a First High student was kidnapped," Mikihiko interjected. "We can't just let this slide."

"Right." Leo nodded.

Unlike Mikihiko, Leo wasn't in a position where he had to worry about other students. But no one was insensitive enough to comment on that.

Instead, Honoka spoke up: "Shizuku. Maybe we should contact Tatsuya and Miyuki. Shiina did disappear during her student council duties, after all."

"We should definitely contact *Miyuki*," Shizuku pointedly replied.

"I don't want to bother her." Izumi hesitated, careful not to be her usual fangirl self.

"We could just send a text," Shizuku suggested.

"I'm on it," Honoka replied, and pulled out her mobile device.

Miyuki was at her usual hair salon when Honoka's text message arrived.

The appointment with Mayumi was at 5:00 PM. Since there was plenty of time to spare, Miyuki decided it was the perfect time to get her hair done. Her go-to salon was open to first-time customers, but it was an exclusive location that catered to important people who prioritized security. While its prices were high, the number of clientele was small. That made it possible for Miyuki to schedule an appointment at the last minute. She even made an appointment for Minami as well.

Due to the nature of the salon, it had an area specifically for bodyguards to wait. Tatsuya was reading a digital text in this area behind Miyuki. It wasn't a paper related to FLT business, nor a document related to the Yotsuba family's business. It was solely for pleasure. In other words, it was safe to say that—despite his friends' supposed concerns—Tatsuya was not busy at all.

Miyuki's device rang. The tone, a little different from usual, signaled that someone close to her had an emergency. Unable to reach the device herself, Miyuki called out to her fiancé.

"Tatsuya?"

He looked up from his text. "Yes?"

"Could you check my terminal, please?" she asked.

"Sure. Did you get an email?" he said, rummaging through her purse.

"Yes. I think it's urgent."

Tatsuya wasn't insensitive enough to peek at Miyuki's private messages, but he also wasn't reserved enough to refuse to look at them when Miyuki asked. He took her mobile device out of her purse and brought up her text messages.

"It's from Honoka," Tatsuya reported. "She says Shiina disappeared from school."

"What?"

Miyuki jolted so abruptly that the hairdresser warned her, "Please don't move your head, Miss."

The owner of this kind of salon was very good at pretending not to hear. Tatsuya was even willing to read the text message aloud, because he trusted the hairdresser's tight lips.

"Apparently, a man and woman looking like military personnel came to see Shiina, and after that she disappeared without a trace. Honoka says it's possible she followed them somewhere."

"She wasn't kidnapped, was she?" Miyuki asked cautiously, trying to keep her head still.

"They could have forcibly convinced her to go with them, but I doubt they used violent means," Tatsuya reasoned. "If they had, it would have set off the school's security system."

Miyuki knew how First High's security had been strengthened after the terrorist break-in two years earlier. At this point, it was on par with government systems, making it virtually impossible to kidnap a student.

"Should we return to school?" Miyuki questioned.

"Even if we went back, there's nothing we can do," Tatsuya said. "And in the case of a kidnapping, it would be up to the police to decide what's best."

Of course, he wouldn't be talking like this if Miyuki had been kidnapped. Not that there was much chance of that ever happening.

"Do you think the police will act?" Miyuki asked.

"Normally, the fact that we can't say for sure it was a kidnapping would make things difficult," Tatsuya explained. "But Shiina is one of the Mitsuya family head's daughters. I'm sure they have some connections to the police. Besides, it seems Erika is involved in this, too."

"She is?" Miyuki asked, surprised.

"Yeah," Tatsuya said. "And for some reason, Leo and Mikihiko are with her."

"Are you sure you want to leave this in their hands?" Miyuki asked again.

She was mainly concerned that they weren't helping, but it didn't seem to bother Tatsuya at all.

"We're busy," he reminded her.

"That's true."

Tatsuya's statement was perfectly reasonable. Miyuki would have agreed even if he hadn't been the one to say it. What worried her was how their friends would react to Tatsuya's judgment.

Meanwhile, at the Mitsuya family home, Gen, the head of the family, and his eldest son, Motoharu, were holding a secret meeting.

"Father, it seems Shiina was taken," Motoharu reported.

"I see," Gen replied.

As soon as Saburou reported Shiina's disappearance, both Gen and Motoharu immediately recalled their conversation with Tsukasa a few days ago. The description of the person Shiina met also fit Tsukasa to a T.

"Saburou doesn't seem to know Tsukasa is the one responsible," Motoharu continued.

Gen sighed. "That's because he has never met her."

"Really?" Motoharu asked in surprise. This was hard to believe, given how close Tsukasa was with Shiina.

"That woman is extra careful about who she meets face-to-face," Gen explained. "It's probably because of the role the Tooyama clan plays. The fewer people who know what she looks like, the better."

"But she and Shiina have met up so many times. How could Saburou never have seen her face?" Motoharu asked.

"That goes to show how skilled she is," Gen said. "And it's not only Tsukasa. The entire Tooyama family is adept at this type of covert maneuvering."

"I thought Lab Ten specialized in anti-physical and anti-magic barriers," Motoharu puzzled, but Gen shook his head.

"It started off that way, but due to the special nature of its magic activation, the Tooyama clan was given a role that goes beyond mere defense. They were incorporated into the counterintelligence unit of the National Defense Force's Intelligence Department."

"But doesn't every family cooperate with the military in some way? I'm pretty sure our family reports anything noteworthy in East Asia."

Gen shook his head again.

"What the Tooyama clan does isn't simply cooperation. They have completely become a part of the Intelligence Department and wield hidden influence within it."

Gen paused, and Motoharu gulped, waiting for his father to continue.

"Sure, the Tooyama don't have bottomless power like the Yotsuba. The Juumonji can probably best them in magic, even though they both stem from the former Lab Ten. They don't even have the political power that the Saegusa possesses. But because they bear no fame, they also bear no infamy. The Tooyama are a family devoted to the shadows and will stop at nothing to realize the interests of the faction they've chosen."

Gen let out a substantial sigh and continued.

"They would be applauded if were acting in the interests of the country, magicians, or the twenty-eight families. Unfortunately, they are only invested in themselves. The fact that they don't make themselves out to be such an obvious threat as the Yotsuba makes them an even bigger headache."

"Maybe this is an opportunity," Motoharu ventured.

"What do you mean?" his father asked.

"Well," Motoharu began, "right now, the Tooyama clan is practically begging the Yotsuba clan to fight them by targeting Tatsuya Shiba. If it escalates to the point where hostilities break out, we might be able to rid ourselves of the Tooyama once and for all."

"I guess it *is* possible…" Gen hesitated. "But even if the two families fight, there is nothing we can do about it. We will have no choice but to sit on the sidelines."

"But isn't that ideal?" Motoharu insisted. "We will get what we want without having to lift a finger."

"That sounds like a temporary fix. But it's better than the alternative," Gen admitted.

I doubt Shiina will come back to us until some kind of peace is made between the two families anyway, Gen thought with a resigned scoff.

The large sedan that picked up Shiina was both spacious and comfortable, possibly even more so than a limosine. After leaving the First High parking lot, it drove all the way to Karuizawa without using a car train (the train version of a car ferry), which was a rare feat these days when traveling long distances.

They eventually arrived at an old Western-style mansion. Its appearance made everyone who saw it wonder how such a relic still survived in this day and age. In fact, it looked straight out of a horror film. Shiina involuntarily shivered when she got out of the car.

"You must be cold," Tsukasa said. "Come on inside."

It was already the later part of April. Even in Karuizawa, the temperature weren't that low. But there was no point in standing outside, so Shiina followed Tsukasa into the mansion.

"Wow!"

An unconscious gasp escaped Shiina's lips. The mansion's ancient exterior was juxtaposed with an opulent interior that maintained a classic appearance. Tsukasa led Shiina to her room, which was just as luxurious as the lobby.

"This will be your room," Tsukasa said. "Feel free to use it as you like."

Shiina's eye was especially drawn to the large canopy bed at the center. The dresser was also beautiful with its intricate golden details. Shiina was, to some extent, used to living with luxurious things, but she couldn't even begin to fathom how much the furniture in her room could cost.

"The closet is filled with clothes that should probably fit you perfectly," Tsukasa continued. "We're only planning to stay one night, but I figured you still need some clothes."

"Yes, I do. Thank you," Shina replied, ripping her gaze from the room's furniture.

"You're very welcome," Tsukasa said with a smile. "Since you're helping us out here, I had to give you *something* in return."

"Tsukasa?" Shiina hesitated to ask, but ultimately mustered up the courage. "I'm not allowed to call my family, right?"

"No, I'm sorry," Tsukasa replied. "Just think about it as being part of the job."

"All right." Shiina's heart sank, but she had a feeling this would be the case.

"I'll call you when dinner is ready."

With that, Tsukasa left the room. There was no sound of a door locking, but Shiina found it too intimidating to make sure. She had left her bag in the student council room, but her mobile information terminal was tucked into her blazer pocket. She took out the terminal and checked if there was a signal.

Of course there wasn't.

I accepted this job. I can't back out now, she told herself.

She opened the closet and slipped out of her uniform. Then she changed into some casual loungewear and dove on top of the canopy bed.

Shiina wasn't aware that Tsukasa had forced her brother and father to agree to this situation. She felt bad about not telling the student council members and Saburou about it, but she was convinced that Tsukasa had already notified her family. She could never have imagined everyone thought she was missing.

After reading the reply text message, Honoka was overwhelmed with a blend of confusion and disappointment.

"What does Miyuki say?" Erika asked.

"It's actually from Tatsuya," Honoka said, unable to hide the shock in her voice. "He says we should leave the matter to the police."

Erika looked as shocked as Honoka. "Seriously? That's a surprisingly normal thing to say."

"Let me see," Shizuku said, leaning over Honoka's shoulder to view her display.

For the first time in a while, she furrowed her brow.

"It does *say* we should leave things to the police, but we should explain everything," she said.

"Right." Honoka nodded.

She transferred Tatsuya's message to a bigger screen for everyone to see.

"Let's see here…" Leo said, peering at the screen. "It seems Tatsuya thinks there's a good chance Mitsuya was tricked into going with the person she met."

"But there isn't any proof, so we don't know if the police will actually start a search," Mikihiko finished. "That's probably true."

Both boys frowned.

"The message keeps going," Kasumi said. "If Shiina's case turns out to be serious, the Mitsuya family will probably contact the police, so we should leave it to them. Obvious, much?"

"But that is probably the wisest decision. Now that the incident has left school gounds, there's only so much we can do," Izumi consoled her angry sister.

"What if we leave things to the police and they're too late?!" Kasumi yelled.

"Then tell me, Kasumi, what do you propose we do?" Izumi asked calmly. It was most likely her twin's emotional reaction that allowed her to keep a cool head.

"We could use our family's search network!" Kasumi proposed.

"Our father is in Kyoto right now," Izumi said slowly. "Do you know who to contact and what to ask?"

"No, but… We could ask Mayumi to do it for us!"

"Mayumi is out with Shiba."

"That's perfect! I can give that guy a piece of my mind!" Kasumi ran out of the student council room.

"Wait! Do you even know where they went?!" Izumi groaned. "I'm sorry, Mitsui. I need to go now!"

She ran after her twin. Shizuku shook her head and turned back to the remaining members of the group surrounding the large screen.

"Honoka, mind if we leave this here?" she asked.

"Sure, that's fine," Honoka replied, realizing Monday was not going to be fun for Kasumi.

"So what are we supposed to do?" Leo asked. "Sit back and twiddle our thumbs like Tatsuya said?"

Erika scoffed. "We can leave things to the police, but there's no way I'm sitting back and twiddling my thumbs."

"What are you planning to do?" Mikihiko asked cautiously. He wasn't anxious because he didn't know what she was going to do. He was anxious because he knew exactly what she was planning.

"Isn't it obvious?" Erika said. "My family dojo is filled with police officers."

"I believe that's usually called an abuse of power," Shizuku said.

"I don't know about this," Mikihiko groaned.

"If we have people we can rely on, we ought to do just that," Erika asserted.

In the past, a mischievous grin would have spread across her lips. But today, she wasn't smiling.

Mayumi had invited Tatsuya and Miyuki to a traditional Japanese restaurant in Akasaka. It was the kind of place that usually only served customers three times the group's age. On top of that, customers were usually famous, high-class, wealthy, or all of the above.

Tatsuya, Miyuki, and Minami arrived at the restuarant about

three minutes before the appointed time. The waiter showed the three out-of-place guests to their table with a smile pasted on his face.

It was exactly 5:00 PM when the group entered the tatami room to find only Katsuto awaiting their arrival.

"Were you waiting long?" Tatsuya asked, taking a seat without permission.

"No, you're right on time," Katsuto said in a neutral tone.

With rhythmic timing, Miyuki took a seat on a cushion right next to Tatsuya, and Minami sat directly on the tatami mats behind Miyuki. All four of the people in the room were kneeling on the soles of their feet in the traditional fashion. None of them restlessly squirmed in place or wriggled their toes. Everyone seemed to be accustomed to sitting on the floor.

Just as Tatsuya's and Katsuto's eyes met, the sliding door opened and Mayumi and Mari scrambled in.

"Sorry! Did we keep you waiting?" Mayumi said.

"No, we just got here ourselves," Tatsuya said without pause.

A bitter expression appeared on Katsuto's face. He looked like he was about to say something but ultimately stayed silent. Mayumi let out a sigh of relief and knelt next to Katsuto and in front of Miyuki. Mari sat beside her friend.

Compared to most college girls, Mayumi's posture was presentable, but she seemed slightly more awkward than Tatsuya, Miyuki, and Katsuto. If anything, Mari's posture was more elegant.

"Let's get started, then."

Mayumi was about to begin the discussion, or persuasion, session when a woman's voice came from the other side of the sliding door.

"Excuse me."

"Come in," Mayumi responded.

The doors slid open to reveal not a waitress but the restaurant's young proprietress.

"There is someone here who claims to be with your party, ma'am," she said to Mayumi, with a perplexed look on her face. Her confusion was understandable, since everyone invited to this gathering was already in the room.

"Who is it?" Mayumi asked with the same level of confusion.

"Kasumi and Izumi Saegusa," the proprietress replied.

"What?!" Mayumi gasped before turning to Tatsuya and Miyuki. "Excuse me for a second."

She scrambled to her feet and ran toward the restaurant entrance. The proprietress gave the group a polite bow and closed the door behind them.

Miyuki turned to Tatsuya and whispered, "I wonder if they are here because of the incident."

"What incident?" Mari asked. "Do you know why Mayumi's sisters are here?"

Katsuto frowned at Mari's gossip-like question, but Tatsuya didn't seem to care.

"Yes, actually," Tatsuya said. "The youngest Mitsuya daughter was taken today. The Saegusa twins are probably here to talk about that."

"Taken?" Mari asked, surprised. "Do you mean Shiina?"

"Yes, do you know her?" Tatsuya replied.

"I've met her a few times through Mayumi," Mari explained. "Isn't this her freshman year at First High?"

"That's right."

"So what do you mean by *taken*?"

Tatsuya summarized everything he knew about the incident.

"That's an emergency if I ever heard one!" Mari exclaimed. "What are you two still doing here?"

She couldn't believe the student council president and the de facto top student council member were sitting here doing nothing when a First High student might have been the victim of a crime.

"I'm not sure what you mean," Tatsuya replied with a sarcastic smile. He was their guest. It didn't seem fair that Mari was criticizing him when she was one of the people who invited him here.

"Shiba," Katsuto said.

"Yes?" Tatsuya replied.

"Can I put our family business aside for a moment and speak to you as your First High senior?"

"Of course."

Katsuto's voice suddenly became louder. "Let's postpone this discussion. I need you three to prioritize finding that freshman."

Tatsuya's sardonic smile only deepened.

"Juumonji, you and Mayumi Saegusa called me here as a representative of the Yotsuba family. Therefore, if you postpone this discussion, you do so as a representative of the Juumonji family and a member of the Ten Master Clans."

Tatsuya's critique made Katsuto swallow his words.

"If you truly want to postpone this meeting, neither Miyuki nor myself have any objection," Tatsuya asserted.

He glanced at Miyuki, who gracefully bowed her head to signify her approval.

"That said," he continued, "I don't see a reason for you to postpone at all."

"What do you mean?" Katsuto asked.

"It's still uncertain whether the Mitsuya incident is truly a crime," Tatsuya explained. "It is, however, clear that Mitsuya left First High. All the police would have to do is use their authority to check the public road surveillance cameras to see where she went."

"If it's that easy, why don't you do it?" Mari blurted out angrily.

"Because Mitsuya might have acted of her own free will," Tatsuya replied calmly. "Yes, she was taken away, but if she went willingly, sending help would only put us on the wrong side of the law."

"That's rich coming from the guy who invaded the Blanche headquarters," Mari said bitterly. Neither Tatsuya nor Miyuki reacted to her words. They knew Mari was mostly upset because she couldn't logically refute Tatsuya's decision.

"During the Blanche incident, it wasn't even necessary to confirm the willingness of the parties," Tatsuya said.

As Mari gnashed her teeth in frustration, Tatsuya turned back to Katsuto.

"There is nothing we can do *legally* as First High students," he continued. "However, I will not stop you if you still would like to postpone this meeting."

Katsuto crossed his arms and fell into thought. Just then, the sliding doors were flung open.

"I misjudged you, Shiba!" Kasumi yelled.

Mayumi came running after her sister. "Hold on, Kasumi!"

A pale-faced Izumi was panting close behind. "Miyuki, Shiba, I'm so sorry about this!"

"Come on, Kasumi. Be a dear and go home," Mayumi said, as if talking to a small child.

But Kasumi adamantly fixed her gaze on Tatsuya.

"Shiina would never run off somewhere without telling us!" she shouted. "Are you really just going to abandon her?"

Tatsuya couldn't simply say yes to this. Instead, he met Kasumi's question with another question: "Were you listening to our conversation?"

"You better believe I was!" Kasumi yelled, red in the face. "That's right! I was eavesdropping! Bite me!"

"It's not nice to eavesdrop," Tatsuya replied plainly.

"Why, you—!" Kasumi snarled angrily.

"But it does help speed things up," he said. "Shiina is underage. Even if she consented to whoever took her, her guardians still have the right to call the police."

"What's your point?" Kasumi snapped.

"Kasumi," Izumi said firmly, grabbing her twin's sleeve, "his point is that you're talking to the wrong person."

"What do you mean?"

"You should be talking to Shiina's family, not him," Izumi persisted.

"I still don't get it!"

Izumi grabbed her sister's entire right arm. "Come on, Kasumi. We got Shiba's advice. Let's not bother them anymore."

"Right," Mayumi said, grabbing Kasumi's left arm.

"Wh-wh-what are you doing?!" Kasumi squealed.

"I'm so sorry, Tatsuya and Miyuki," Mayumi apologized. "I know I was the one who invited you here, but do you mind if we put a pin in this? I promise to make it up to you."

"Sure. Don't worry about it," Tatsuya replied in a friendly way. Everyone recognized it was no longer possible to have a serious conversation.

"Come on, Kasumi," Mayumi cajoled.

"Let's go," Izumi echoed, and the two pulled their sister away.

Tatsuya and Katsuto looked at each other and sighed.

Then Miyuki spoke up for the first time, bowing to Juumonji. "We look forward to seeing you again soon."

"I'm sorry about this," Katsuto apologized. There was nothing more he could say. Mari remained silent. The meeting of the Yotsuba, Juumonji, and Saegusa came to an unproductive end.

It was almost 6:00 PM, and the sun was about to set. Erika and Leo had left school and arrived at the Chiba dojo. Mikihiko showed up a few minutes later, guided by one of the dojo's pupils.

"Sorry to keep you guys waiting," he said.

"Did you make sure Mizuki made it home safely?" Erika asked.

"I walked her all the way to the door," he replied shyly.

"Great," she said indifferently. She couldn't care less about Mikihiko's schoolboy romance.

He changed the subject. "Any progress on your end?"

"We have some people checking the public road surveillance cameras as we speak."

"Oh, good idea. A car parked at First High School could easily be tracked, even if they used a car train. I wonder why we didn't think of that sooner."

Mikihiko meant this as self-criticism, but Erika simply scoffed.

"It actually wasn't our idea," Leo explained. "We got a text message with the suggestion from Izumi."

"Izumi? I guess I shouldn't be surprised," Mikihiko said, reevaluating the twins' capabilities.

"Actually, Izumi got the idea from Tatsuya," Leo admitted.

"Ah." Mikihiko nodded. Now the brains behind the plan and Erika's attitude made sense.

Leo was under the impression that Tatsuya had given the order to search the surveillance cameras even though this wasn't the case. Then again, no one present knew this, and it was inconsequential.

"Thank you. I appreciate it. Goodbye."

Saburou suddenly appeared, hanging up on a call.

"What did the Mitsuya family say?" Erika pressed.

Saburou frowned in a mix of despair and anger.

"Both Shiina's father and Motoharu claim there's no need to panic," he said.

"Who's Motoharu?" Leo whispered.

"Mitsuya's older brother," Mikihiko whispered back.

"This is *really* strange. Something is off," Saburou muttered, scratching his head in confusion. "Sure, Shiina's family has always given her a lot of freedom, and she never had a curfew, but that was only because she had a full-fledged bodyguard with her. Someone who wasn't me. I don't understand why no one is panicking when no one knows where she could have gone!"

"Is there no chance they secretly have a bodyguard shadowing her?" Leo ventured.

Saburou firmly shook his head. "I already asked my family about that. At this point, Shiina is one hundred percent missing."

Erika seemed pensive, but she simply asked, "So what are you going to do?"

"I want to wait here," Saburou insisted. "That's why I came."

"All right. Do what you want." She shrugged.

The dojo was starting to get busy. It was only a matter of time before the adult training classes started, and Erika's father would be one of the teachers.

"The three of you, come with me."

Erika strode out of the dojo without waiting for a reply. She led the group to the small, distant building where her room was. The sliding door she opened was so low that all three boys had to duck to pass through. The group entered a four-and-a-half tatami Japanese-style room with a furnace toward the back. A hanging scroll decorated the small alcove on the side.

"Wow, I didn't know you had an authentic tearoom," Leo said, impressed.

"Hilarious, right?" Erika scoffed. "It's like we're your typical samurai family. Even though the swordsmanship we teach isn't traditional at all."

Mikihiko frowned. He knew this was a jab at her family, not at herself. Leo, on the other hand, was either oblivious to this or decided to play dumb.

"I always thought tearoom entrances were smaller than this," he said.

"You mean the kind you have to enter on your knees? There's one over there if you want to try it out."

She pointed to a smaller entrance on the other side and walked behind another sliding door. Then she appeared again with four cups of tea on a tray and said, "Stop standing around. Have a seat."

Erika gracefully dropped to her knees and set the teacups on the tatami. The three boys obediently each sat in front of a teacup. They stared at her as Erika took a sip of tea and suddenly looked up.

"What? Were you expecting me to perform a traditional tea ceremony or something?"

The three boys quickly shook their heads. She glared at them in turn.

"There's no way I would go to all that trouble."

"Ha-ha, right…" Mikihiko laughed, with a hint of disappointment.

Erika ignored him and took another sip of her tea. A few minutes passed in silence. Somewhere in the middle, Erika stood up to bring the group a pile of thin-skinned steamed buns. The rest of the time, all four of them were mostly quiet—minus the sound of them chewing their steamed buns.

It was almost 8:00 PM when a new sound broke the relative silence.

"Miss Erika."

A young man's voice called from the other side of the smaller door. Erika quickly rose to her feet and slid the smaller door open. The man handed her a thin electronic paper. She brought the terminal with her back to the center of the room.

After she finished reading the document, Mikihiko ventured quietly: "Any news?"

"It seems we've found the car that drove Shiina."

Saburou slammed his hands on the tatami mats and raced to Erika's side. No one told him to calm himself. Everyone in the room knew he had been dying to hear this.

"It went directly to Karuizawa," Erika continued.

"That's closer than I thought," Leo mumbled, clearly implying that they should have found her sooner.

"The process always takes time," Erika reminded.

What she meant was it took a while before her people could get access to the surveillance camera data.

I'm just saying, Leo seemed to say with a shrug.

Erika placed the electronic paper in the center of the group so everyone could see.

"Is it just me or does that mansion look haunted?" Mikihiko murmured.

"That's not funny, Miki," Erika warned, even though she secretly agreed with him.

Saburou gazed eagerly at the image. "Can I have the location information?"

"Sure," Erika said. "But you're not allowed to go there today."

"Why not?!" he protested.

With the level of impatience to get to Shiina's side, Erika knew he wouldn't be immediately receptive to what she was about to say. But she stood firm.

"Two reasons," she said. "First, you're not ready."

"I can be ready in two seconds!" Saburou argued.

"Are you really planning to go out there alone?" Erika sighed. "Give it up. You're digging your own grave."

Saburou realized this meant the whole setup could be a trap meant for him. Yet he persisted: "But we finally found her."

"No, we didn't," Erika said firmly. "All we know is that the car Shiina was in is parked in this mansion's driveway. Don't worry, we have a tracker on it now in case it moves."

"……"

Erika glanced at Saburou before continuing. "Second, we haven't made contact with the police yet. I don't mind going to jail as a last resort, but I will *not* make a fool of myself just because I'm unprepared."

Her mention of jail made the long-haired boy fall silent. He would gladly give his life for Shiina, but he couldn't force Erika and the others to do the same. Besides, this was increasingly looking like a task he couldn't accomplish alone.

"I want you to go home and talk to your family," Erika ordered. "In the best case scenario, the Mitsuya promise to help. But even if they don't, you need to get their tacit approval for us to act on our own."

"All right," he agreed.

Erika was right. Saburou's actions could affect his family, and the Mitsuya clan by extension. He reminded himself that he was not in a position to act freely.

◇ ◇ ◇

Around that time, Shiina was taking a relaxing bath.

"I bet Saburou is worried sick about me," she sighed.

The guilt she felt for leaving school without telling Saburou handily outweighed the responsibility she felt for leaving the student council members. It felt like there was a tiny fish bone caught in her throat and it wouldn't come out. Now that the bath had calmed her nerves about being in a new place, these feelings of guilt once again bubbled to the surface.

Then again, there was nothing she could do. Tsukasa had begged her to keep it a secret for the sake of the nation. Shiina convinced herself that it wasn't too surprising that a top-secret exercise meant she was forbidden to communicate with the outside world. Of course, she had no idea why they would hire a high school student to work part-time on an exercise like this, but she wouldn't dare disobey Tsukasa's instructions.

It wasn't easy saying no to an adult almost ten years her senior who was practically begging for help. Trying hard to justify her own decisions, Shiina put her worries aside and tried to relax in the bath.

Unfortunately, this Western-style mansion where she was basically being kept under house arrest didn't have a hot spring. What it did have was an antique claw-foot bathtub.

Perhaps because it was designed for Westerners of a larger build, it was considerably larger than a standard Japanese bathtub. It was even long enough for Shiina to comfortably stretch out her legs. So much, in fact, that she was worried she might drown if she wasn't careful.

Shiina smelled a faint aroma mixed in with the steam, possibly from a fragrant oil dripping into the water. The smell seemed to melt away the very core of her soul. For a moment, Shiina wondered if the smell came from some kind of drug, but the thought quickly disappeared.

Needless to say, Shiina always took off her earmuffs during a bath. As a result, even the sound of the shower rinsing her hair felt

like listening to a torrential downpour, but there was nothing she could do about it. Her magical ability decreased at times like these, so she used magic to block her hearing while washing her hair and body.

Once she was ready to soak, it was actually freeing to face the raw world without any filter as long as she was careful not to make any unnecessary splashing. Not only was her acute sense of hearing at its full potential, but her magical perception was also sharper than usual. Simply resting her head on her arms on the edge of the bathtub allowed her ears to be bombarded with the vibrations of the entire Western-style mansion.

A female soldier stood watch in front of the bathroom door. Shiina could sense the faint psion waves she emitted via her CAD on standby. Clearly, this soldier was a combat magician, but she wasn't the only one.

Everyone moving around the mansion—women and men alike—were all magicians with their CADs on standby. It was as if they were prepared to transition into combat at any minute.

Of the five soldiers patrolling the outside of the mansion, however, only one was a magician. The psion waves he emitted were also more restrained than those of the military personnel stationed inside. Perhaps this was their way of hiding the fact that there were magicians inside the mansion. Shiina grasped all of this while casually lounging in the tub.

Of course, this wasn't all. She also noticed the waves the magicians in the mansion were emitting felt substantially aggressive. It was almost as if they were awaiting an enemy, and their purpose was either to kill or to capture.

This did not conflict with the information Tsukasa had relayed when Shiina first accepted the job. The older woman had asked her to play the role of a VIP in need of rescue for the sake of a military exercise. In other words, the main team would play the role of the rescuer.

Her supposed kidnappers were probably the ones in the house right now on the lookout for an attack. Shiina felt her treatment was too generous for a kidnapped prisoner of war, but she figured it went along with her status as a VIP.

Just then, she realized something important. As someone in the role of a hostage, she had no idea when the rescue team would arrive. It might even be now. If she wasn't careful, the rescue team might even walk in on her wearing only a bath towel.

This was no time to be taking a leisurely soak. Shiina stood up with her hands on the sides of the tub as fast as she could without making too much noise.

As soon as Tatsuya, Miyuki, and Minami returned to the house, their videophone rang. The caller ID read Maya Yotsuba. Fortunately, they had just returned home, so they were still fully dressed. Tatsuya and Miyuki exchanged glances and accepted the call.

"*Good evening, my dears,*" Maya greeted in her superficially friendly fashion. "*Oh, have you been out?*"

"Yes, Mayumi Saegusa invited us to a restaurant," Tatsuya replied honestly. He didn't see the need to hide it.

"*So it was an invitation from the Saegusa clan?*"

"Not exactly. The head of the Juumonji clan was there, too, so they probably wanted to talk to us about the Youth Council."

"*That sounds like something Mayumi would do,*" Maya chuckled.

Tatsuya could agree she was just that naive.

"Unfortunately," he continued, "something came up. A few minutes after we arrived at the restaurant, our meeting was canceled."

"*How rude,*" Maya mused. "*What happened?*"

Takuya summarized the entire Shiina incident.

Once he was finished, Maya responded, "*Fascinating. It's too bad I don't have more time to talk about it.*"

This meant she had urgent business to attend to. It was always about work whenever Maya called the Shiba household herself.

Neither Tatsuya nor Miyuki was surprised. They simply waited politely for their aunt's next words.

"*We have found that the people who attacked you earlier were a group of American soldiers who entered Japan without authorization. The National Defense Forces' Intelligence Department brainwashed them and were using them as puppets,*" she reported.

"So Intelligence was behind this," Tatsuya murmured. This wasn't surprising to him after Yakumo's warning, but the Yotsuba clan's ability to discover this in a single day was nothing short of impressive.

"*It seems that a number of USNA military operatives are still being held captive,*" Maya continued.

Tatsuya wondered what those operatives came searching for in the first place. There was a high possibility they were after the magician responsible for Material Burst, aka himself. But he was hesitant to interrupt his aunt just to confirm this.

"*I'd like you to rescue those operatives,*" Maya said.

"You mean the Americans?" Tatsuya asked, slightly surprised.

He couldn't forgive the Intelligence Department for attacking Miyuki and was planning to make them pay for it one way or another. Then again, it was the Intelligence Department's duty to detain foreign operatives engaged in illegal activities. The Yotsuba clan shouldn't be allowed to interfere with this simply for the sake of retaliation.

"*Yes,*" Maya said. "*Some of the operatives are Stars members.*"

Tatsuya had expected this. In fact, he believed almost all of the USNA operatives the Intelligence Department had captured belonged to the Stars.

"*Rather than rescue a handful, I'm sure it would be much easier to simply release them all,*" Maya continued.

"Understood," Tatsuya replied.

Clearly, some kind of relationship had been established between Maya and the Stars. It was through that relationship that the Stars requested a rescue mission.

Now the Yotsuba clan's best interests and Miyuki's best interests were connected. Tatsuya was willing to do anything the situation called for. As part of his promise the previous night, he decided to accept Maya's orders.

The morning after Shiina's debatable kidnapping, Leo, Mikihiko, and Saburou stopped by the Chiba dojo. After some warm-ups, Erika spoke to Saburou.

"Did you talk things over with the Mitsuya clan?"

"Yes," he responded. "They said they didn't care what I did."

"O…kay."

This was clearly the same as retracting their permission, but Erika shrugged. It was important for Saburou to express his purpose. Anything after that was his responsibility.

Erika turned to the other two boys. "I knew Leo would want to join in on the fun, but I didn't expect you to show up, Miki."

"For the last time, my name is Mikihiko," he said as per routine. Once that was out of the way, he continued with the utmost sincerity, "Well, I came this far. I can't just turn my back on you guys now."

"Aw, you're such a softy," Erika teased.

"Yeah, yeah. It's better than being coldhearted," Mikihiko retorted.

"Touché. Well, let's get this show on the road."

Erika climbed into the passenger seat of a police car parked in front of the dojo. As soon as the three boys packed themselves into the back, the car took off.

"I know I should have asked this sooner, but are you really okay with this, sir?" Leo asked the uniformed officer in the driver's seat.

"This isn't the first rodeo Miss Erika has taken me on," the officer answered with a deadpan expression.

It seemed to Leo that the officer's response was not a result of his devotion to Erika; he genuinely considered this all quite normal. Leo secretly vowed never to let this happen to him.

*   *   *

The police car took a car train to Karuizawa—which was much faster and more economical than taking the highway—and met up with the local police. Needless to say, all of the officers were the Chiba clan's people. Leo wondered at that moment whether the Chiba clan wasn't actually more terrifying than the Yotsuba clan. But he didn't have a death wish, so he didn't say this out loud.

Saburou was too preoccupied with the case at hand to have the luxury of having these kinds of thoughts. He glared at the old Western-style mansion that he had seen in the previous day's report. Or perhaps he was trying to use magic to see through its walls.

Meanwhile, Erika was busy giving instructions to officers. This made Mikihiko the most mentally relaxed of the group. It was only natural he was the first to spot a couple of familiar faces.

"Kasumi? Izumi? Is that you?" he blurted out when he spotted them.

The twins simultaneously spun around. Although their hair and personalities were completely different, their facial features were uncannily similar.

"Well, if it isn't Yoshida," Izumi said.

"I see Chiba, Saijou, and Saburou are all here, as well," Kasumi added.

They stepped away from the group of adults they had been talking to and walked over to Mikihiko.

"Are you here because of Mitsuya?" the older boy prompted.

"Yes," Kasumi replied.

A lot was abbreviated in this question and answer, but both parties understood the situation perfectly.

"Well, we don't want to bump heads trying to do the same thing. Why don't we discuss our plans?" Erika called out from behind Mikihiko.

"Good idea." Izumi nodded. Kasumi seemed to agree. Erika had a point.

Mikihiko and Leo, however, felt something was off. The Erika they knew was rarely this rational and cautious. Up until the previous year, Erika tended to abandon the rules, preferring the thrill of an aggressive frontal attack.

Something was really off.

Both Leo and Mikihiko realized the way she was handling the situation at hand was very similar to how Tatsuya might approach this. That said, it was pointless to interfere. As Erika suggested, the situation called for coordination if they wanted to avoid friendly fire. Though still finding Erika's behavior rather unsettling, Mitsuhiko and Leo joined the discussion.

By the time Shiina opened her eyes again, it was light outside. As she regained consciousness, an unbearable rush of noises bombarded her ears. She quickly put on her earmuffs.

Shiina's abnormal hearing was only functional when she was awake. Whenever sleep overtook her, sounds regained their normal volume. This helped prove the hypothesis that her acute hearing was caused by magic use.

It looks like there weren't any rescue missions last night, Shiina thought, regaining awareness of where she was.

Tsukasa had told her that her part-time job wouldn't last more than half a day, but those plans had clearly been extended.

Shiina was suddenly overcome with hunger. But not so much that her stomach rumbled. She decided to change into her uniform, so she would be ready for whatever awaited her.

The room—or series of rooms—she was in on the second floor was almost like a luxury hotel, complete with a bath, toilet, and dressing room. After slipping on the dress part of her uniform, she went to the dressing room to carefully blow dry and style her troublesome hair. There, she found a makeup set, which for some reason was the same brand she used at home. After using magic to check for any harmful substances, she quickly went through her makeup routine.

That was when the commotion started. Shiina heard people running through the hallways. She put her hand to the doorknob to see what was going on, but the antique knob didn't budge.

I'm locked in?! ...Oh, wait. Of course I am, she thought. Her instinctual surprise soon melted away when she remembered her role as the kidnapped VIP.

It's okay, she assured herself.

Her CAD hadn't been confiscated, so she could use magic without any problem. If push came to shove, she could easily break through a window or the ceiling to escape. The fact that she even considered escaping was proof that something was beginning to feel strange about the situation she was in. Nevertheless, she forced herself to overcome her doubts about Tsukasa and remain a damsel in distress for a little longer.

Meanwhile, she decided to distract herself with innocuous thoughts like *I'm starving...*

"Restablishing camera surveillance!" a soldier announced.

"Is that the SMAT police force? Why would the police be after us?"

The second lieutentant—who was again only superficially in charge of operations—exclaimed with an incredulous look on his face. The police force he mentioned was called the Special Magical Assault Team, or SMAT for short.

SMAT was a police unit of combat magicians put together after the police's failure to respond to the Yokohama Incident two years prior. Although the decision to establish this unit was made immediately after the incident, opposition to it arose from all sides once the cease-fire with the Greater Asia Alliance was established. As a result,

SMAT had only officially started operating fairly recently in response to the Hakone terrorist attack in February.

It was a pitiful organization in a sense, as the mass media was still being very crtical of the unit. It was even under scrutiny from the upstart Nonprofit Press (NPP) about its slow start. That said, its members maintained a high morale, seemingly turning their bad reputation into motivation. Their most significant feature was that almost all of them were members of the Chiba dojo.

The second lieutenant appointed to command the operation was of a different section than Tsukasa. That meant he was unaware of the operation's motives behind the scenes. In fact, he wasn't aware of its public motives, either. Witnessing SMAT troops surround the Western-style mansion, however, should have been a big hint.

It looks like the troublesome Chiba tomboy got involved, Tsukasa thought with a sigh.

She had foreseen the possibility that Tatsuya and Miyuki wouldn't be the only ones drawn in by using Shiina as bait. Tsukasa knew the Saegusa twins' love for Shiina would cause them to join the rescue mission. That's why she was coordinating with her superiors to keep Kouichi Saegusa in Kyoto.

As expected, only a few Saegusa magicians had appeared outside the mansion. This alone wouldn't have thrown a wrench in the operation. The Saegusa clan *plus* the Chiba clan's involvement was an entirely different story.

Truth be told, the Chiba clan—though a major disruptive factor—was not a true threat to the operation. It was a different miscalculation that could potentially make the operation lose meaning entirely.

I don't see Tatsuya Shiba. Did he not take the bait? Tsukasa thought. *That could be a problem.*

I thought he would be more egoistic, but he's unexpectedly petty.

A younger student had just been kidnapped from the school where the Yotsuba heiress served as student council president. Tsukasa had thought Tatsuya would surely come to rescue the hostage so as not to lose face.

Based on what she observed during the attack on Miyuki's finishing school, she had concluded that Tatsuya had absolute confidence in his own abilities. People like him tended to prioritize their reputation above all else. The only case in which they would willingly risk that reputation would be if they anticipated defeat.

It seemed, however, that Tatsuya Shiba didn't care much about his reputation at all. Tsukasa admitted that she had miscalculated. Through Tatsuya's process of rescuing Shiina, Tsukasa had hoped to observe how much he valued state power. If he showed little regard for the National Defense Forces' authority, she had planned to name him a potential threat to the state and propose his removal.

Unfortunately, at this rate she wouldn't be able to observe how Tatsuya would act, knowing he would have to oppose the National Defense Forces.

"Things didn't go my way. But that's how real life goes sometimes," Tsukasa muttered, neither pessimistically nor with a sigh of defeat. She walked straight up to the commanding second lieutenant.

"Captain."

"How can I help you, Sergeant Tooyama?" he replied.

"May I have permission to go monitor the POW?" she asked.

The term "prisoner of war" meant something very specific during wartime. However, it was not uncommon in the military to use *POW* to refer to someone held captive, simply out of habit. In the past, even captured enemy horses were sometimes recorded as prisoners of war.

In this situation, the second lieutenant unsurprisingly mistook Tsukasa's term to refer to the girl being held captive in the mansion. In other words, Shiina.

"Permission granted," he said.

"Thank you."

Tsukasa did intend to go to Shiina's room first. But she was not going to stay there. She had asked for permission to escape to the place where the USNA soldiers were being held captive—though they were not technically prisoners of war, either.

As a rule, unlawful combatants were not considered prisoners of war until their captors recognized them as such. But Tsukasa shelved this minor detail into the back of her mind.

"We will begin the raid in three minutes."

"All right. I'll leave you in charge."

"I'm honored."

The SMAT section commander Erika had been speaking to flashed her a bold smile. He used to be the head of the Erika Secret Service force at the Chiba dojo. Remembering that he knew all sorts of things about her, Erika shyly turned away.

On the other side of the area, the Saegusa twins were gazing nervously at the mansion with their family's magicians around them. Erika worried about their anxiety but knew this was normal. A few minutes ago, they had told her this would be their first real battle. They had dealt with a few more-or-less powerless activists before but had never faced an armed enemy.

They may be magic high school students, but like most normal high school students, they didn't usually engage in actual combat. Erika and her classmates, who had been dodging bullets on battefields ever since they entered First High, were decidedly the odd ones out.

In the midst of all the chaos she had to face, Erika even joked that she imagined high school as a more boring place. Looking back now, she realized this was not a joke at all.

An armed terrorists' invasion of the school, a Greater Asian Alliance surprise attack, an encounter with the parasites and Stars, domestic ancient magic magicians working for foreign powers—these were all disturbances Erika and her classmates had faced. She had not been the cause of any of them. In some way or other, she had just become involved.

The same could be said for Tatsuya. But Erika saw a pattern. Whenever there was an incident, Tatsuya got involved. Whenever Tatsuya was involved, Erika got involved. Wherever Tatsuya went, bad luck was always close behind.

But it was never a big deal until her family got involved.

"Erika, is something wrong?" another male SMAT member looked at her, concerned.

She shook her head. "It's nothing."

Like the section commander, this man had also been a member of the Erika Secret Service.

She changed the subject. "Isn't it time to start soon?"

"Yes, in twenty... Make that fifteen seconds."

I won't let bad luck get the better of me, Erika thought. *I'll get stronger. Then again, it's not enough for me alone to be strong.*

I've brought my own share of bad luck. Just last summer, I involved my parents in a situation of my own. Tatsuya is strong. That's why he has never minded getting involved. Once you're strong, you don't even have to worry about fate. By avoiding tragedy, I clear away that bad luck.

If Tatsuya is a bringer of bad luck, I can make those around him stronger. I'll make them strong enough to laugh off the bad luck.

Saburou, you need to get strong soon. So strong that you can laugh your way out of the bad luck your childhood friend has caught you up in.

Erika spoke this sililoquy from the heart to the long-haired boy who looked like he was about to jump toward the mansion at any second. She could tell just by looking at him that he was trying his best to hold back.

She felt that Shiina Mitsuya was born under a bad star. Shiina wasn't as bad as Tatsuya, but she felt those two were sort of like kindred spirits.

Erika swore to toughen Saburou against the bad luck Shiina might inadvertently invite upon him. She considered Saburou's training an experiment for her ultimate revenge. Her target was none other than fate itself.

Shiina's head popped up at the sound of her door unlocking. To her relief, it wasn't her imagination.

"Tsukasa!" she exclaimed.

"Hi, Shiina," Tsukasa greeted. "Sorry for keeping you locked up for so long."

"That's okay," Shiina replied. "This room has been very comfortable."

"I'm glad to hear that."

Tsukasa smiled without the slightest hint of guilt and continued: "We're now in the final stages of the exercise, so I would appreciate if you could stay here a little longer. There has been a slight mishap, and we're behind schedule, but we can wrap things up once the rescuers get to this room."

"So we won't be moving anywhere?" Shiina asked.

"That's right," Tsukasa replied.

Shiina was overcome with relief. She didn't doubt Tsukasa received her parents' consent to do this little side job, but she was afraid they would worry if she was away longer than originally promised.

"I'm going back to my post and won't be able to say goodbye, but hang in there," Tsukasa said.

"Oh, of course," Shiina replied. "Thank you for your hard work."

"It's a bit early to say this, but thank you for your help, too." Tsukasa smiled.

Shiina didn't doubt her to the very end.

The battle between the National Defense Force and the police, the Intelligence Department, and SMAT had begun. Although it was a battle, the number of people on either side was small. The police maintained control over the area and sent in a few of their best men. The National Defense Force did not have that many soldiers. But they made up for that with high combat skill.

So far, the two sides had been fighting each other with nonlethal weapons, and many SMAT members had dropped out of battle.

"Violent Wind Sutra!" Mikihiko yelled.

Then Leo bellowed, "Panzer!"

Amid all the fighting, Leo and Mikihiko stood above the rest. Mikihiko wielded a mass of wind as a mallet and called forth a translucent orb of wind to ram into the barricade. Meanwhile, Leo, clad in hardened magic armor, jumped in when his opponents were scattered.

"Shiina! Where are you?"

As Saburou shouted and charged forward in the same way as Leo, he was attacked by a military magician who emerged from behind the barricade.

The soldier, clad in urban camouflage and a bulletproof vest, used self-acceleration magic to unleash a series of sharp kicks while simultaneously using teleportation magic to hurl small metal spheres through the air.

Saburou was stopped in his tracks as a steel sphere the size of a Ping-Pong ball hit him in the stomach. The military magician then pulled out a stun baton. Unlike commercially available batons, this one was designed for combat.

Just as the baton closed in on Saburou's neck, Erika appeared out of nowhere. *Wakizashi* in hand, she struck the soldier directly in the face with the blade's edge.

The blow was more like the crack of a whip than a large swing. It wasn't strong enough to make broken teeth spew from the soldier's mouth, but his body collapsed from underneath itself.

"Saburou, stop rushing!" Erika warned. "You're getting sloppy!"

"Right! Sorry!" the long-haired boy replied.

The Intelligence team must have thought this was the critical moment. They concentrated their forces at the top of the stairs leading up to the second floor.

They excelled in both combat and magic. In fact, their magic surpassed that of SMAT, whose magicians were prized more for their exceptional combat skills.

"Mikihiko," Leo called out, "is it just me, or is something off about these guys?"

"They might be using drugs to temporarily boost their magic!" the disciplinary committee president replied.

It wasn't until the two boys were directly involved in the battle that they realized their opponents had been drugged.

"Then how am I supposed to…hit them?!" Leo yelled.

Erika used her *wakizashi* to deflect several incoming rounds. Magic alone was troublesome, but now the police force was having a particularly hard time dodging these bullets being shot at them from a few meters away.

The bullets' initial speed was 200 kilometers per hour, at best. Each round was made of large, light materials, so they had relatively short range. Because of the rapid decrease in speed as they flew through the air, they also couldn't penetrate their target. These bullets could break bone at close range, but at a distance of two meters, they would only leave a bruise or light burn.

The problem was the burns. As soon as a bullet hit its target, it generated a high-voltage current that rendered a person immobile, even if it didn't punch through their clothes.

In other words, each bullet was a lot like a wireless taser gun. Both the National Defense Force and the police were hesitant to kill a fellow Japanese authority figure. That made firearms incapable of killing overwhelmingly superior in terms of ease of use. Especially since both sides were on par with each other in areas such as magic, having a weapon that didn't hold them back could be a deciding factor in the battle's outcome. It only took two petite girls protected on all sides to disrupt this balance.

"Let's do this, Izumi!"

"Right behind you, Kasumi!"

Erika, Leo, and Mikihiko immediately swerved out of the way.

"Three."

"Two."

"One!"

"Cast!" the twins chanted together to synchronize their magic.

A violent wind raged in a small area of the room. Just as the wind blowing down from overhead seemed to hold down both targets and allies, it hit the soldiers and policemen crowded in the small zone from multiple angles.

The only ones who were able to stay standing under the raging wind were those who succeeded in quickly deploying airtight magical barriers.

"Nitrogen Storm!" the twins yelled in unison.

The military magicians were suddenly incapacitated by hypoxia from exposure to air with a significantly increased nitrogen density.

"Next!" Kasumi shouted.

The Saegusa twins' multiplicative cast was a collaborative spell where one sister constructed the magic program and the other provided interference power to activate a single spell. Kasumi and Izumi could use magic in exactly the same way, but in many cases, Kasumi was responsible for the magic program and Izumi was responsible for the interference. That meant Kasumi decided what kind of spell to create.

This time, she chose Dry Blizzard. This spell gathered carbon dioxide particles pushed away by the activation of Nitrogen Storm and made it fall as dry ice hail. Even airtight shields couldn't block individual pieces of dry ice. At this point, there were no National Defense Force soldiers left standing.

"Kasumi!" Izumi yelled.

"I know!" her twin replied.

The last spell they cast was Oxygen Chamber, which literally referred to oxygen capsules. It was a spell for treating hypoxia by creating an area of highly concentrated oxygen.

"Yoshida, Saijou, please restrain the enemy!" Izumi called out.

The police officers who had collapsed from Nitrogen Storm regained consciousness and got to their feet. Leo, Mikihiko, and other police officers who happened to be out of the twins' magic range restrained the National Defense Force soldiers who had not been granted Oxygen Chamber and were still lying on the ground.

"What...just happened?"

Saburou also finally recovered from his semiunconscious state. He unsteadily walked over to Erika.

"Those two are cunning little monsters, aren't they?" she muttered under her breath.

"What?"

"Oh, nothing."

Erika couldn't help but notice that the twins were clearly taking every opportunity to steal the spotlight. But she quickly hid her cynicism when Saburou asked her about it.

"Let's go find Shiina," she said instead.

"Right."

Leaving cleanup to the police, Erika and Saburou headed farther along the second floor. A female soldier was standing in front of a room from which they sensed Shiina's presence.

Erika pointed her weapon at the soldier. Just as she was about to cast self-acceleration magic, the soldier dropped her CAD weapon and raised both hands in the air.

"Does that mean you surrender?" Erika asked.

She didn't expect a reply, but the soldier nodded immediately.

"Yes, I surrender. As a result, this exercise has ended in a victory for the rescuers."

"What exercise?"

Neither Erika nor Saburou knew what this meant. But before they could even begin to understand, the soldier unlocked the door behind her. Immediately, Saburou moved into the room in search of Shiina. His eyes swept the interior. But he heard her voice before catching sight of her.

"Saburou?!"

"Shiina!"

Saburou took a few brisk steps forward and suddenly froze. Realizing his body was unconsciously moving to embrace his childhood friend, he willed himself to stop. But he couldn't stop himself completely. Instead, he limited himself to a distance of an arm's length.

"What are you doing here?" she asked, gazing at him with large eyes.

"I'm here to save you, Shiina!" he exclaimed. "Are you hurt? They didn't do anything terrible to you, did they?"

"Save me? But why?" she asked again, looking truly mystified.

Saburou couldn't believe his ears. "Have you been brainwashed?"

"I'm sorry. I just really don't know what you're talking about," Shiina said slowly. "I was just helping the National Defense Force with one of their routine exercises."

Saburou's mouth dropped open.

"What?" he gasped.

Erika turned to the female soldier who had put her hands in the air again after opening Shiina's door.

"Mind explaining what all this is about?"

She aimed the tip of her sword at the soldier with a dangerous look in her eye.

"Is this question aimed at me, your prisoner?" the soldier asked, her voice calm.

"Obviously!"

"Then please lower your sword. The laws of war forbid soldiers from intimidating their prisoners with threats of physical harm."

"Well, aren't you a piece of work!" Erika snapped, raising her voice.

But the soldier's steady gaze convinced her to reluctantly lower her sword.

"Better?" Erika grumbled.

"May I also lower my arms?" the soldier asked.

"Fine."

Without changing her expression, the soldier dropped her arms behind her back in an at ease position and began to explain.

"The task of this exercise was to rescue a VIP. Our forces were divided into a rescue team and a defense team. The rescue team was originally tasked with taking the civilian playing the role of the VIP from this mansion to the designated location by 18:00 today. However, due to a mishap on the rescue team side, the conditions were changed so that exercise ends when the rescue team reaches this room."

Erika brought her free left hand to her forehead.

"You mean to tell us Shiina has been playing the role of VIP?"

"Affirmative. Miss Mitsuya has been helping us since yesterday."

"You do know we're not members of the National Defense Force, right?"

"I do. However, we were not notified that the exercise had been suspended, so we continued the exercise, despite your participation."

"Grrr!" Erika ruffled her hair in frustration. "You can go now. I'm not your enemy, so you're not my prisoner."

"Excuse me, then." The soldier saluted Erika and jogged down the corridor. The fact that she remained unarmed proved there was no hostility on her end.

"What a huge joke this is," Erika muttered to herself.

Saburou turned to Shiina, still in disbelief. "Is all of that true?"

"You mean about the exercise?" she asked. "Yes, it's true. Tsukasa asked me to help out the soldiers."

"Who is Tsukasa?"

"Tsukasa Tooyama, the chief of the National Defense Force's Intelligence Department. Haven't you met her? She comes by Lab Three quite a lot."

"Never heard of her."

"Anyway!"

Shiina suddenly realized something important and thrust herself into Saburou's face.

"What possessed you to interrupt the military exercise? You could have been seriously hurt! Besides, you're acting like you did nothing wrong, but what if you get arrested for obstruction of official duties?"

"That's not going to happen," Erika interjected.

"Chiba..." Shiina's cheeks flushed with embarrassment as she remembered the third party in the room.

"The National Defense Force, on the other hand, started a full-blown battle in the middle of a city without receiving permission to carry out this exercise in the first place. If anyone is going to get arrested, it would be them."

"Following that logic, couldn't you all get arrested for joining in that full-blown battle?"

"No, our actions were fully sanctioned, since we were cooperating with the police. By the way, Mitsuya, I'm surprised you know who I am."

Just because they were cooperating with the police didn't mean they could go waving weapons around. But Erika didn't have a trace of guilt on her face. While she was speaking, she suddenly realized that this was the first time meeting Shiina face-to-face.

"Of course I know you. You're famous among the freshmen. Oh, and you don't have to be formal with me. Please call me Shiina."

"All right. Shiina, then. I'm not trying to defend what Saburou has done, but I want to let you know there's a reason behind his actions. You see, we all thought you had been kidnapped."

"What?!" Shiina froze.

After a few seconds, she turned to Saburou and asked, "Really?"

"Yes!" Saburou exclaimed. "Chiba isn't even the only one who came with me. Kasumi, Izumi, Mitsui, and Kitayama are all here, too. We've all been really worried. You caused a whole fiasco."

"I don't believe it..." Shiina whispered. "Tsukasa said she informed everyone."

"Don't worry. We don't blame you for what happened," Erika said. "Someone clearly sweet-talked you into this."

"Oh…"

Feeling like she was being called gullible, Shiina let out an adorable whimper. Luckily, Erika wasn't the sorority big sister type with a soft spot for younger girls, so things didn't get awkward in a strange way.

"Anyway, the truth of the matter is that you caused a lot of concern, so you should apologize for that," Erika continued.

"You're right. I'm sorry, Chiba."

Shiina obediently bowed her head, making even Erika's firmness soften.

"No need to apologize to me. I'm talking about Honoka, Shizuku, and the twins."

"Oh, right. I'll apologize to them later, then."

"What a pain," Erika muttered under her breath.

Shiina wasn't quite an airhead like Mizuki. In fact, she was in such a category of her own that it made her hard to deal with. Luckily, Shiina didn't hear this last part.

Erika continued. "Mind if I change the subject?"

"Sure," Shiina said.

"Did I hear you mention the Intelligence Department?"

"Yes, that's the organization Tsukasa works for."

"Interesting," Erika mused. "Not that it means anything."

It may have just been a result of preconceptions, but Erika sensed something suspicious in the air.

[7]

This Sunday was the first in a long time that Katsuto didn't have Ten Master Clans duties. He quickly completed his Magic University assignments in the morning, had lunch, then relaxed with some vinyl records.

His classic analog recordings were part of the only thing he could call a hobby. Analog records were relatively expensive in the late twenty-first century, but they were in constant demand among enthusiasts. Even now new recordings were made every year, mainly of orchestral performances.

Katsuto was one of these enthusiasts. He never felt inclined to build an audio soundproofed room, though. Blocking out all noise felt unnatural to him. He preferred outdoor concerts in nature to concerts in fancy halls.

So he opened up his room, leaning back on a firm sofa and listening to his favorite symphony on his hi-fi system. Despite the old-fashioned appearance, it was packed with the latest technology to reproduce an enhanced version of an old sound.

To tell the truth, while Katsuto loved both chamber and solo performances, he preferred his music live. Unfortunately, he had neither the time to learn to play an instrument nor the time to hire a performer. None of the members of the Juumonji clan, in fact, had much time on their hands. They were much too busy acquiring and maintaining their tremendous power.

"Sorry to bother you, son."

"Oh, hi, Dad."

Katsuto's father and former head of the Juumonji clan, Kazuki Juumonji, walked through the open doorway. He was only forty-four years old, an age much too young to retire. But the cost of playing the Juumonji family's fated trump card had forced him to leave his position and hand the reins over to Katsuto at the Master Clans Council in February.

"Lord Tooyama is here," Kazuki announced.

"Lord Tooyama?" Katsuto repeated.

The only person Kazuki called "Lord Tooyama" was Shinobu Tooyama, the head of the Tooyama clan. Katsuto immediately lifted the needle off the record and headed to the parlor, wondering why Shinobu, and not Tsukasa, had come to visit him.

Tatsuya had arrived near the tip of the Boso Peninsula. From the mountain road, he used his Third Eye to observe a prisonlike facility on the opposite slope. This was the location of the magicians he was charged with rescuing.

Tatsuya had received Maya's orders the night before. But he didn't leave his home until after lunch this day. He never intended to blindly follow Maya's orders, nor did he feel the need to do so. His late departure, however, wasn't for emotional reasons. He didn't feel the need to disobey his aunt this time. The reason he was running late was simply because he didn't know where to go. At the time of Maya's call, neither she nor the Yotsuba clan had located where the USNA agents were being held.

Tatsuya returned to the box truck that Hyougo Hanabishi had been driving him around in. Hyougo surprisingly had a license for driving large trucks. He laughed when he said he also had a license for operating heavy machinery, but he probably wasn't kidding. Tatsuya figured Hyougo could even fly a large passenger plane if there was an occasion to.

Hyougo was the one who provided information about the location of the USNA soldiers. Over the phone, he only gave Tatsuya a meeting place location. This was probably more to convince the younger boy to ride in his truck and less to avoid any eavesdropping.

When Tatsuya reached the truck, Hyougo was not in the driver's seat. He was outside of the truck, waiting. As soon as Tatsuya nodded, Hyougo quickly went around to the back of the truck and unveiled a large, box-shaped cargo bed. It appeared to be some sort of aluminum but was actually made of a composite-armored version of titanium alloy and ceramic.

With the click of a remote control, one of the back doors slid open, revealing a small boarding ramp.

"After you," Hyougo offered.

Tatsuya stepped into the back of the truck. It wasn't as dark as he had thought it would be. The lights were probably set to automatically turn on as soon as the ramp came down. The cargo bed interior looked like a small laboratory. On the side, there was a black, fully cowled electric motorcycle and what looked like a riding suit on a hanger.

"Is that a MOVAL suit?" Tatsuya asked.

"Good eye, Master Tatsuya," Hyougo smiled. "I'm surprised you recognized it at first glance."

Tatsuya was the one who was surprised. He automatically began analyzing the suit's performance with his Elemental Sight.

"I didn't expect to see such a perfect replica of an Independent Magic Battalion MOVAL suit in a place like this," Tatsuya said in awe.

"Oh, it's not perfect at all," Hyougo rebuffed. "We ultimately had to forego the original suit's power assist function."

Tatsuya of course knew that much, but he was still starstruck by the design. He was especially amazed by the suit's ability to connect to his Third Eye.

"However, disposing of the power assist allowed us to enhance this suit's defensive and stealth capabilities to a level higher than the original. I'm proud to say that this one should even prove more user-friendly for you to operate."

MOVAL suits were developed by the Independent Magic Battalion, but they did not exclusively belong to the National Defense Force. The USNA military even developed a thrust suit—a flight-armored suit with the same functions as the MOVAL suit—three months after the Independent Magic Battalion's design.

The Yotsuba clan, however, was undoubtedly the first to develop flight-armored suits in the private sector. Even discounting the fact that flight magic was originally developed at FLT, which was under the Yotsuba family's management, it was still an amazing technological feat.

"I almost forgot to mention," Hyougo added. "This motorcycle can link to this flight suit."

"You mean it can fly?" Tatsuya asked.

Hyougo nodded. "Exactly."

Tatsuya turned his Elemental Sight to the motorcycle. It had no protection against side or rear attacks due to its shape, but it had as much defense as an armored car from the front. The motorcycle's build, including its tires, was also extremely sturdy. Although disguised as a commercial vehicle, it was clearly made for combat.

"Master Tatsuya, the suit doesn't have a name yet. I would be honored if you could give it one," Hyougo said with an expectant look.

"No thanks," Tatsuya declined. Even though this reveal had completely taken him by surprise, he wasn't completely won over. If he ended up giving the suit an embarrassing name, he was the one who'd be most embarrassed by it when he put it on.

There was no need to ask. The suit was obviously for him. The Yotsuba clan must have anticipated the rift between Tatsuya and the

Independent Magic Battalion, which naturally affected his access to a real MOVAL suit.

Tatsuya's weakness was his low defense. He had nearly unstoppable regenerative powers, but he couldn't always rely on them immediately during battle. In some cases, he had to prioritize destroying his enemy. For this reason, high-performance defensive clothing was an indispensable piece of equipment for Tatsuya to achieve his full potential.

Unlike regular MOVAL suits, this suit was comfortable enough to wear on the street. Even with a helmet, it only looked like a slightly bulky motorcycle riding suit. If he wore a jacket on top, it would almost look like a normal outfit. This flying suit seemed to be made for Tatsuya. In fact, it probably was.

"Then for the sake of convenience, we can temporarily call it the Freed Suit," Hyougo suggested. "If you ever think of a better name, I would love to hear it."

Tatsuya was perfectly fine with Hyougo's suggestion. The name *Freed Suit* meant a suit free from constraints. Tatsuya wondered why Hyougo didn't choose the name *Free Suit*, which was basically the same thing, but it was probably just a matter of word choice.

Not wanting to waste time with unnecessary questions and answers, he kept quiet. Ultimately, the name was inconsequential. Tatsuya needed this suit. He thanked Hyougo and began putting it on.

Unlike the suit, the black motorcycle already had a name: *Wingless*. Though it had no wings, it could still soar. Tatsuya found this name rather tasteful.

Straddling *Wingless*, Tatsuya headed for the prison where the USNA soldiers were being held. This time, he was on his own. Hyougo stayed back at the meeting point in case of an emergency. If things turned sour, the plan was for the USNA soldiers to steal a car at the prison and make their escape.

Even without a backup team, Tatsuya wasn't worried. His fighting style was actually more suited for battles of one against many. A lack of support also meant no allies to protect. All he had to think about was himself, and he was free to use his full combat potential.

Tatsuya kept to the legal speed limits to avoid any unnecessary trouble, but he still arrived at his destination fairly quickly. As if testing out a new toy, he used his new motorcycle to soar over the prison wall.

Tsukasa Tooyama did not move from the Western-style mansion in Karuizawa to the secret prison on the Boso Peninsula because she had a plan for the USNA army magicians. It was simply an excuse to get out of a pickle. She wanted to disappear before Shiina and her uninformed colleagues could begin to ask questions.

Prisoners that couldn't be brainwashed were of no use to Tsukasa. If she persevered and continued to administer the drugs, she might yield results. But before that happened, it was highly probable that the soldiers' magic skills would be lost, their personalities destroyed. Tsukasa was not so inhumane as to go around destroying people without restraint. At least, that was what she thought.

The USNA soldiers she captured would probably be disposed of. Since they infiltrated another country as unlawful combatants, they should have been prepared for the consequences. Releasing them was out of the question. Survivors would reveal that the Japanese military created puppets out of their prisoners through chemical brainwashing.

Executing prisoners was one thing. But if the Japanese military was found guilty of human experimentation, it would lead to a world of trouble.

Things would be a lot easier if Tsukasa could simply turn herself in, but that wouldn't be enough. It was imperative to avoid anything that might disadvantage the National Defense Force and, by extension, Japan. Without Japan, there was no Tooyama clan, and without the Tooyama clan, there was no Tsukasa Tooyama.

As the saying went, an idle mind is the devil's workshop. This wasn't completely the case this time. But people did tend to start thinking bad thoughts when they had nothing better to do. This tendency was especially strong among people who were usually busy.

"If I'm going to get rid of something, the sooner the better," Tsukasa muttered, alone in a room. This room was a waiting room for the jailors, but they were currently on duty at their posts.

The room where the soldiers were confined was completely airtight. If a lethal chemical was poured into the air conditioning, it could be turned into a gas chamber. She stood up to petition the prisoners' execution to the prison warden.

Just then, the alarm went off.

"What's going on?" she murmured.

A soldier rushed in, answering Tsukasa's question.

"Chief Tooyama, there's an intruder! Please get ready!"

This soldier was a sergeant. After confirming he was of a lower rank, Tsukasa pressed him about the situation.

"How many intruders are we talking about? Can the guards handle it?"

"There was only one confirmed intruder, but it's a powerful magician! The guards can't stop him!" the soldier reported.

An impossible thought flashed through Tsukasa's head, but she quickly dismissed it as delusional. The Yotsuba clan should have no reason to attack the prison.

"All right. Where is my equipment?" she asked.

"It's waiting for you here."

The sergeant offered Tsukasa a pair of full-shield sunglasses with an information terminal function and a headset with a microphone that covered only one ear. The sunglasses displayed the coordinates of the intruder and information on the soldiers moving to intercept him.

Allied soldiers were within normal range.

"I'm going in as support," Tsukasa said, and activated her Tooyama family magic.

Tatsuya located where the USNA agents were being held with the terminal in the first security room he stumbled upon. Then he destroyed the HVAC system, just to be safe.

What kind of holding facility locks their prisoners in a gas chamber? he wondered.

Tatsuya had a bad feeling about the prison when he first arrived. Now he was almost certain it was an illegal research facility.

That means there's no need to hold back, he mouthed silently.

Luckily, he hadn't been planning to hold back from the very beginning. The facility was located in a mountainous area with no trace of civilians around.

He pointed his CAD pistol at the security guard in front of him. The suit he was wearing had a fully thought-operated CAD preinstalled, but for this battle, he chose to use a familiar pistol form. His weapon was a Silver Horn Custom Trident, equipped with a specialized CAD that instantaneously produced the activation program.

It allowed him to activate dispersion quicker than usual, puncturing the soldier in his path. It wasn't lethal, but the fallen soldier would not be able to crawl, let alone stand again. Of course, he quickly fainted from the excruciating pain.

A new enemy appeared.

Tatsuya tried to add on an attack mechanically. The soldier, appearing from the corner of the corridor, was clad in an anti-magic barrier, but he was no stronger than the soldier before him. Tatsuya attempted to disintegrate the magic barrier and promptly follow that up by hitting the soldier's body. However, immediately after he disassembled the barrier, it was reassembled in a matter of seconds.

The soldier countered with a high-power rifle.

Tatsuya used magic to instantly disassemble its bullets and quickly escaped from the line of fire with the help of his suit's power. But there was nothing in the corridor to hide behind.

He disassembled a section of the ceiling and jumped through the hole. Three soldiers chased after him.

Using the hole to take cover, he activated Program Dispersion.

The three soldiers' anti-magic barriers dissipated only to immediately reappear. The next moment, the barriers dissipated once again. Then Tatsuya's dispersion spell punched holes in the soldiers' bodies before the barriers could be reinstated.

He destroyed six barriers and wounded each soldier four times. This meant a total of eighteen event modifications, but it wasn't a difficult exercise at Tatsuya's current level.

He was more fixated on the reconstructing magic barriers.

It isn't Phalanx, he thought.

The Juumonji family's spell, Phalanx, was well-known for its ability to continuously generate magical barriers. However, Tatsuya had seen Katsuto's Phalanx before. He was sure the spell he was witnessing now involved a different technique. It was uncannily similar, but not the same.

I bet it's another spell created in Lab Ten, he thought.

He dropped through the hole in the ceiling and proceeded down the corridor again.

That could only mean one thing. The Tooyama family is involved.

Now that he thought about it, this magic barrier spell was identical to the one he saw during the attack on Miyuki's etiquette school. Which meant the Tooyama family was behind that attack, too.

Maya told me not to get involved, Tatsuya thought. *But if the other party is trying to harm Miyuki, I have no choice.*

All the other soldiers who appeared in Tatsuya's path were clad in the same magic barrier, but they couldn't block his advances any longer.

It's an annoying spell, he thought, *but it actually works well with me.* As he calmly evaluated his enemy's magic, Tatsuya finally entered the area where the prison cells were.

I can't believe this! My—no, the Tooyama family magic isn't working against him!

Tsukasa screamed internally as she assisted the battling soldiers.

The Tooyama family's magic functioned by simultaneously projecting multiple personal magic barriers. In other words, it was a technique that built a magic barrier around the physical body of the target.

Since this target was registered in advance, there was no need for direct visualization or resetting coordinates. The magic barrier could be applied to as many people and as many times as the caster's capacity allowed.

The Tooyama family technique was originally intended to assist in the escape of important persons. The spell was designed to help key government officials get to safety, protecting them from bullets and explosions in case of an enemy attack.

The Tooyama family was the central government's last line of defense. Meanwhile, the Juumonji family served as the capital's last line of defense. A government was not a building, but the people who governed. Allowing the people at the top of the chain of command to escape provided the opportunity for a swift counterattack. The Tooyama family magicians were developed with this idea in mind.

The Tooyama family was meant only to protect key government officials. Regular citizens were not included. Because of this, Tooyama magicians were not meant to appear in the spotlight and, while included in the twenty-eight families, they never tried to make a name for themselves.

Though their magic was developed with the extremely passive motive of providing a means to abandon the citizenry and escape, this did not mean it couldn't be used to proactively stop enemy soldiers. When a Tooyama family member targeted an ally's identification signal and activated the spell, a soldier could concentrate solely on attacking while clad in a barrier more powerful than anything they could muster themselves. The soldier didn't even have to be a magician to benefit from the barrier.

Tsukasa wore a visor developed by the Intelligence Department precisely to allow her to break away from being a magician only for the sake of escape. Deep down, the Tooyama family yearned to contribute to the nation in a positive way.

Since they could only activate their magic around others, the Tooyama had the inherent—or implanted—flaw where the boundaries between their own identity and several others' became ambiguous.

Yet they aspired to contribute to the organization to which they belonged. Perhaps it was because of the ambiguity of their individuality that they felt a strong need to contribute to a group.

To fulfill this need, the National Defense Force's Intelligence Department struck a deal with the Tooyama family under a pseudonym. Tsukasa was the second generation trapped in this deal. Now she had become an integral part of the Intelligence Department.

Whenever a country tried to sabotage another, the sabotage team usually included magicians. Magic was an exceptionally powerful force that an individual could wield. Inevitably, counterintelligence programs put in place to prevent sabotage required the ability to counter magic.

Since the Tooyama family's magic provided non-magicians with magical barriers, this gave them a significant advantage in counterintelligence.

Soldiers defending their bases relied heavily on Tsukasa's magic. If they discovered that her magic didn't work, it would greatly reduce their morale, and their defense could completely fall apart. This was why Tsukasa couldn't show anxiety on her face.

Due to a congenital defect, Tsukasa's ability to experience anxiety had been impaired, so it was not difficult for her to maintain a poker face. But performance aside, the consequences of her inability to stop her target were dangerously apparent.

The USNA soldiers were confined to a block surrounded by a spiral corridor. If the cells had been a separate building, Tatsuya could have easily entered it from the outside. But as things stood, it was as if a courtyard had been built inside a building and the prison had been erected inside the courtyard. This forced Tatsuya to go to the trouble of dealing with guards as he worked his way in.

Once at the holding cells, there was no longer any need to obediently proceed through the hallway. Tatsuya pointed his Trident at the inner wall and used demolition magic to blast a series of holes through the barrier. Suddenly, there were holes big enough for people to pass through in all the prison walls.

He then pointed his Trident at the ceiling, dropping plaster chunks on the guards below. Using his Elemental Sight, Tatsuya saw the guards' anti-magic barriers quickly switch to object barriers. While this guaranteed there were no casualties, getting out from under the rubble was still a struggle.

It was perfect for Tatsuya.

He ran to the holding cells. The fact that no one had escaped even though the doors were wide open could only mean the prisoners were in a state where they couldn't move.

Tatsuya's theory was right on the money, but it was far from the worst-case scenario. The prisoners were luckily only paralyzed by drugs. If their limbs had been amputated, it would have been a challenge to carry all of them out.

He focused his Elemental Sight on the drugs poisoning the prisoners. Fortunately, they had all been administered the same drug. Tatsuya would only have to cast magic once.

He focused on the concept of the drug in question and activated a decomposition spell to break it down at an elemental level. Although some of the resulting elements were harmful to the human body, the spell at least cured the soldiers of their paralysis.

He then called out to a woman nearby who was coughing violently as if on the verge of vomiting.

"Can you stand? I'd like you to tell your comrades we're getting out of here."

"Y-yes, I think I can," she replied. "Wait. Are you…Tatsuya Shiba?"

Tatsuya frowned under his helmet. The suit he was wearing wasn't equipped with a voice changer, but he had thought the helmet at least muffled his voice.

"You know who I am?" he asked.

The only way she could recognize him by his voice would be if they had met somewhere before.

This time she coughed before responding.

"—Yes, I'm warrant officer Silvia Mercury, a member of the USNA's magician unit, the Stars. I was dispatched for a short time to Japan last year as Lina's second-in-command."

"So you're Lina's second-in-command," Tatsuya murmured. "That makes sense."

He didn't get the sense this woman was lying. Military officers on an illegal operation mission didn't reveal their identity so easily. This woman must have already known that Tatsuya was aware she and her comrades were USNA military personnel. While they were confined, their captors must have used drugs on them for interrogation.

Moreover, it made sense that an agent at Lina's side could identify Tatsuya's voice from a few words.

He continued. "I've been given orders to help you escape. Hopefully, you can all walk out of here on your own two legs."

"We can," Silvia assured him. Her nausea seemed to have dissipated, and her coughing had stopped. "I'll gather the others."

* * *

Tatsuya led the way out of the prison. Luckily, none of the USNA military personnel were foolish enough to attack him from behind.

Meanwhile, the guards blocking the path seemed to have lost stamina. Interference became largely sporadic. Tatsuya spotted a truck used to transport soldiers and sprinted up to it. Thanks to their rigorous training, all the USNA soldiers had already recovered enough to run.

Tatsuya punched the address of Hyougo Hanabishi's location into the truck's navigation system.

"The truck's GPS will lead you to one of my men. Follow his instructions, and you should be able to escape the country safely."

Sylvia hesitated for only a moment before nodding.

"I won't ask why you're helping us. You saved us from what under any other circumstances would have led to execution. All I will say is, thank you."

She saluted Tatsuya, who saluted back as per military protocol.

After seeing off the truck, Tatsuya returned to the prison. He could have just escaped.

His riding suit with the smoke-shielded helmet was stealthy enough to prevent identification. And before approaching Silvia, he had smashed all the surveillance equipment in the area, including the hidden microphones.

He had even secured a record of the human experiments conducted at the prison from the security room terminal as insurance. It didn't include the research data itself, but it detailed the destruction of corpses that had been used in various experiments. Even if his identity was exposed, this record was good enough to use as a bargaining chip.

The reason why he was returning to the prison was to preemptively erase all the problematic records so he could avoid the unnecessary trouble later. While this was far from necessary, for personal reasons, it was better to take care of it now.

Tatsuya pointed his Trident at the top floor of the building and cast a decomposition spell to obliterate the command center roof. Then, using his suit's flight function, he dropped into the command center from above. Once inside, he found the prison commander and his staff waiting for him.

"Hands in the air."

"We surrender," the commander said. "We're no match for your combat power."

Tatsuya nodded and responded in a magically synthesized voice.

"Erase all the data from the surveillance system."

This was a flash-cast version of Sylvia's signature magic. He may not have the precise control to reproduce voices in someone's ear due to his limited interference abilities, but he could deliver words inside his helmet or make the air in front of his face vibrate to give the illusion of speaking.

The commander in charge immediately did as he was told.

Tatsuya reached for the nearest terminal. Not bothering to go to the trouble of disguising what he was doing, he used magic to decompose all electromagnetic information.

He looked up to the side and saw the operator giving him a frightened look. Tatsuya barely reacted before turning back to the commander.

"Where is the Tooyama family magician?"

The commander hesitated for a moment but then remembered he was not in a position to refuse to answer.

"Chief Tooyama is in the next room," he replied in a voice tinged with guilt.

Tatsuya couldn't care less about the commander's feelings.

"Don't follow me," he said, and turned off the magic voice synthesizer.

He leaped up and peered into the next room from above. As he suspected, it was empty. From his position in the air, he could see a figure escaping stealthily from the building. They headed toward the same parking lot where he had taken Silvia and the other USNA military personnel. Tatsuya dropped from the sky, blocking Tsukasa's path.

"You must be the Yotsuba clan's Tatsuya Shiba," she said suddenly.

Tatsuya replied with magic, dissipating the magic barrier around the Tooyama magician. Then he raised his right arm and pointed his Trident straight at her. The magic barrier continuously flickered on and off until Tsukasa dropped to her knees in exhaustion.

It took Tatsuya much less time to dissipate the barrier than it took her to make it. Just as he was about to pull the trigger, a shout echoed through the air.

"Wait!"

At the same time, an anti-magic barrier formed around Tsukasa. Its speed and strength noticeably superior to the one Tsukasa herself had made.

Tatsuya was able to dissipate the barrier, but it almost immediately regenerated. This back-and-forth repeated itself dozens of times in the span of three seconds until a figure dropped from a helicopter above.

"I won't let you kill her," the figure said.

It was Katsuto. Tatsuya kept his pistol pointed at Tsukasa, but the older boy intervened.

"I don't know what's going on here," Katsuto said, "but I need you to leave."

He mouthed Tatsuya's name but didn't say it out loud. Tatsuya lowered his Trident.

Katsuto continued. "If you leave now, I promise to let you go unharmed."

Tatsuya nodded in silence and turned away. Unafraid of a possible attack, he activated a flight spell to bring him to *Wingless* and exit the premises.

Before long, Katsuto watched the young magician flying away on a jet-black bike.

[8]

A week after the illegal prison attack, Tsukasa paid a visit to Katsuto's home.

"I apologize for visiting during such a busy time," she greeted with a deep bow as Katsuto entered the parlor. "Thank you for your help the other day."

"You've already thanked me more than enough," he said, implicitly urging her to lift her head.

Tsukasa understood his unspoken words and brought herself upright.

"Please," he continued. "Have a seat."

She sat back down on the sofa as she was told.

"So how are you feeling?" he asked.

"Good as new, thanks to you," she replied.

The battle with Tatsuya had put a heavy strain on her magic-calculation region. There were concerns about serious aftereffects, but luckily, she was back to normal after less than a week's rest.

"I heard it was my father who told you to come rescue me," she said.

"No, he just informed me about a personal dispute between magicians," Katsuto corrected. "It was my duty as a member of the Ten Master Clans to put a stop to it. Please don't feel like you owe me anything."

He had actually saved Tsukasa out of obligation to a fellow Lab Ten clan, but he was used to paying lip service when it was due.

"A personal dispute, you say?" Tsukasa's lips twisted into a slight, sarcastic smile.

The prison attack was completely one-sided, but she was the one who had provoked it, which apparently made it a fair fight. Surely her father had told Katsuto about all of this.

"Then, was the attacker really—?"

"Tsukasa." Katsuto stopped her midsentence. "You don't want to finish that question. Or tell anyone what happened that day. Do you hear me?"

"All right," she complied. "But only because you saved my life."

Katsuto sensed the resistance in her answer but decided against saying anything about it. Tsukasa paused before speaking again with her usual emotionless smile.

"Do you mind if I say something completely unrelated?"

"What is it?" the Juumonji family head asked, without batting an eye.

"Last week's battle made it crystal clear, Katsuto. I believe you can beat him."

At that moment, not even Katsuto could keep a straight face.

Lunch was over, and it was almost time for afternoon tea. Miyuki was at her desk at home, studying for college entrance exams.

With her level of magic, it was impossible for her to fail. Regardless of the recommendation quota alotted to each magical high school, the Magic University would unquestionably ask her to enroll.

However, Miyuki was set on taking the entrance exam like everyone else. She wanted to earn a score worthy not only of the magic department but of the general studies department, as well. This was the only way she believed she could prove herself as a suitable fiancée for Tatsuya.

Just as she came to a stopping point and felt it was time for tea, her visiphone rang. She was about to pick up the call when the ringing stopped. Minami must have picked it up in the living room.

I wonder who it is, she thought.

Suddenly, her visiphone received a forwarded call.

"Who is it, Minami?" Miyuki asked.

Forwarded calls didn't bother showing the caller's face on the screen. Minami's voice on the other end betrayed her confusion.

"It's an international call," she said. "From someone named Lina."

Miyuki gasped, shocked to hear that name. But she quickly pulled herself together and said, "Please connect us."

An image appeared on Miyuki's visiphone of a young woman of equal but different beauty than Miyuki.

"Hi there, Miyuki," she greeted. *"You look good."*

"Hello, Lina," Miyuki replied. "I could say the same to you. But why the sudden call? Isn't it the middle of the night on your side of the world?"

"Yes, it's almost 11 PM," Lina said with a sigh. *"Unfortunately, this was the only time I could talk. My superior gave me special permission to call you, but headquarters can never know."*

"I see. So what is the occasion?"

Miyuki understood the importance of this call. She tried to keep things frank to make it as easy as possible for Lina to bring up a clearly difficult topic.

Lina hesitated. *"Um, is Tatsuya there?"*

"My brother?" Miyuki asked.

The title inadvertently slipped out of her mouth. Most likely because she was speaking casually with someone she didn't usually interact with.

"He is out, actually," she said. "Did you need to speak to him?"

"*Yes, but… Can I leave a message?*" Lina asked.

"Of course," Miyuki cautiously complied. "What do you want me to tell him?"

Lina took a deep breath and sat up a little straighter on the screen.

"*I need you to thank him for me. Without his help, I would have lost my second-in-command and best friend.*"

Miyuki immediately knew what Lina was referring to. Tatsuya had told her everything that happened a week ago. She had a good idea about who Lina's best friend was, too.

She could only imagine how hard it must have been for a person of Lina's position to call a Japanese magician—the Yotsuba family heiress, no less—and tell her all this. But it gave her so much joy to know that the Stars' commanding officer worked up the courage to do it anyway and express her gratitude for Tatsuya's help.

"I appreciate that, Lina," Miyuki said. "I'll be sure to pass on the message."

"*Thanks, Miyuki. I'm counting on you.*"

The two young women spent a brief moment looking at each other.

"*Well, I have to go now,*" Lina continued. "*I wish I could thank Tatsuya in person.*"

"Don't worry," Miyuki replied lightly. "I know that's impossible with your position."

"*You've got that right.*" Lina chuckled.

Miyuki paused before adding, "I look forward to seeing you again someday."

"*Me too,*" Lina said. "*See you later.*"

"Yes," Miyuki nodded. "Very soon."

They intently gazed at each other's faces until the screen faded to black.

(*To be continued in the* Isolation Arc)

Afterword

You have just finished reading Volume 22, *Upheaval Prologue Arc II*. Did you enjoy it?

While the previous volume focused on an increasingly tense global situation, the main theme of this volume revolved around our protagonists' changing circumstances. This unbalanced structure was a result of splitting the plot originally intended for a single volume into two. Ultimately, I have no one to blame but myself.

Also, the cliff-hanger in Volume 21 leads to Volume 23, rather than Volume 22. I hope you're ready to see even greater changes take place. The story from Volume 21 onward has transitioned from being divided into distinct arcs to being more strongly connected by a continuous narrative.

Saburou and Shiina, the new freshman duo, seem to have taken the hero and heroine positions in both Volume 21 and 22, but they will settle into regular supporting character status from Volume 23 onward. I know. It seems like such a waste.

Much like the Kuroba twins, Saburou and Shiina would make great subjects for a spin-off. Unfortunately, I don't have time to write that myself. I probably feel this way because I haven't exhausted their full potential. It's a luxurious problem to have.

On that same note, there were two major themes in the conceptual stage of this series. One theme was the conflict between those who can use magic and those who cannot. This is also the current main storyline.

The other theme revolved around the struggle for the heritage of prehistorical civilization, which used magic as its foundational technology. This is much like Hideyuki Kikuchi's "Alien Series" or Hiroshi Takashige and Ryouji Minagawa's *Spriggan*. My own series doesn't draw on well-established occult themes like they do, but I envisioned creating artifacts related to entirely fabricated legacies and ruins. The remnants of that idea can be seen in elements, such as antinite and Relic.

Unfortunately, the series is now at a stage where the end is in sight, so incorporating prehistoric civilization themes into the story at this point is impossible. My only chance would probably be during Tatsuya's and Miyuki's postgraduation stories. As of now, however, the prospect of doing something like that seems unlikely.

As for the next publication, I plan to take a break from my other series and focus on this one. The current tentative subtitle is the *Isolation Arc*.

I hope we'll meet again in Volume 23 of *The Irregular at Magic High School* and look forward to seeing you again soon.

Tsutomu Sato